KING,
QUEEN,
KNAVE

Books by Vladimir Nabokov

Translated by Dmitri Nabokov in collaboration with the author

VLADIMIR NABOKOV

A NOVEL

KING, QUEEN, KNAVE

McGraw-Hill Book Company · New York · Toronto

FOREWORD

Of all my novels this bright brute is the gayest. Expatriation, destitution, nostalgia had no effect on its elaborate and rapturous composition. Conceived on the coastal sands of Pomerania Bay in the summer of 1927, constructed in the course of the following winter in Berlin, and completed in the summer of 1928, it was published there in early October by the Russian émigré house "Slovo," under the title *Korol', Dama, Valet*. It was my second Russian novel. I was twenty-eight. I had been living in Berlin, on and off, for half a dozen years. I was absolutely sure, with a number of other intelligent people, that sometime in the next decade we would all be back in a hospitable, remorseful, racemosa-blossoming Russia.

In the autumn of the same year Ullstein acquired the German rights. The translation was made—competently, as I was assured—by Siegfried von Vegesack, whom I recall meeting in the beginning of 1929 when passing with my wife posthaste through Paris to spend Ullstein's generous advance on a butterfly safari in the Oriental Pyrenees. Our interview took place in his hotel where he lay in bed with a bad cold, wretched but monocled, while famous American authors were having quite a time in bars and so forth, as was, it is often said, their wont.

One might readily conjecture that a Russian writer in choosing a set of exclusively German characters (the appearances of my wife and me in the last two chapters are merely visits of inspection) was creating for himself insurmountable difficulties. I spoke no German, had no German friends, had not read a single German novel either in the original, or in translation. But in art, as in nature, a glaring disadvantage may turn out to be a subtle protective device. The "human humidity," *chelovecheskaya vlazhnost'*, permeating my first novel, *Mashen'ka* (published in 1926 by "Slovo," and also brought out in German by Ullstein), was all very well but the book no longer pleased me (as it pleases me now for new reasons). The émigré characters I had collected in that display box were so transparent to the eye of the era that one could easily make out the labels behind them. What the labels said was fortunately not too clear but I felt no inclination to persevere in a technique assignable to the French "human document" type, with a hermetic community faithfully described by one of its members—something not unsimilar, in a small way, to the impassioned and boring ethnopsychics which depress one so often in modern novels. At a stage of gradual inner disentanglement, when I had not yet found, or did not yet dare apply, the very special methods of re-creating a historical situation that I used ten years later in *The Gift*, the lack of any emotional involvement and the fairytale freedom inherent in an unknown milieu answered my dream of pure invention. I might have staged KQKn in Rumania or Holland. Familiarity with the map and weather of Berlin settled my choice.

By the end of 1966, my son had prepared a literal translation of the book in English, and this I placed on my lectern beside a copy of the Russian edition. I foresaw having to make a number of revisions affecting the actual text of a forty-year-old novel which I had not reread ever since its proofs had been corrected by an author twice younger than the reviser. Very soon I asserted that the original sagged considerably more than I had expected. I do not wish to spoil the pleasure of future collators by discussing the little changes I made. Let me only remark that my main purpose in making them was not to beautify a corpse but rather to permit a still breathing body to enjoy certain innate capacities which inexperience and eagerness, the haste of thought and the sloth of word had denied it formerly. Within the texture of the creature, those possibilities were practically crying to be developed or teased out. I accomplished the operation not without relish. The "coarseness" and "lewdness" of the book that alarmed my kindest critics in émigré periodicals have of course been preserved, but I confess to have mercilessly struck out and rewritten many lame odds and ends, such as for instance a crucial transition in the last chapter where in order to get rid temporarily of Franz, who was not supposed to butt in while certain important scenes in the Gravitz resort engaged the attention of the author, the latter used the despicable expedient of having Dreyer send Franz away to Berlin with a scallop-shaped cigarette case that had to be returned to a businessman who had mislaid it with the author's connivance (a similar object also figures, I see, in my *Speak, Memory*, 1966, and quite properly, too, for its shape is that of the famous *In Search of Lost Time* cake). I cannot say I feel I have been losing time over a dated novel. Its revised text may soften and entertain even such readers as are opposed, for religious reasons no doubt, to an author's thriftily and imperturbably resurrecting all his old works one after the other while working on a new novel that has now obsessed him for five years. But I do think that even a godless author owes too much to his juvenilia not to take advantage of a situation hardly ever twinned in the history of Russian literature and save from administrative oblivion the books banned with a shudder in his sad and remote country.

I have not said anything yet about the plot of *King, Queen, Knave*. This plot is basically not unfamiliar. In fact, I suspect that those two worthies, Balzac and Dreiser, will accuse me of gross parody but I swear I had not read their preposterous stuff at the time, and even now do not quite know what they are talking about under their cypresses. After all, Charlotte Humbert's husband was not quite innocent either.

Speaking of literary air currents, I must admit I was a little surprised to find in my Russian text so many *"monologue intérieur"* passages—no relation to *Ulysses*, which I hardly knew at the time; but of course I had been exposed since tender boyhood to *Anna Karenin*, which contains a whole scene consisting of those intonations, Eden-new a hundred years ago, now well used. On the other hand, my amiable little imitations of *Madame Bovary*, which good readers will not fail to distinguish, represent a deliberate tribute to Flaubert. I remember remembering, in the course of one scene, Emma creeping at dawn to her lover's château along impossibly unobservant back lanes, for even Homais nods.

As usual, I wish to observe that, as usual (and as usual several sensitive people I like will look huffy), the Viennese delegation has not been invited. If, however, a resolute Freudian manages to slip in, he or she should be warned that a number of cruel traps have been set here and there in the novel.

Finally, the question of the title. Those three court cards, all hearts, I have retained, while discarding a small pair. The two new cards dealt me may justify the gamble, for I have always had an ivory thumb in this game. Tightly, narrowly, closely, through the smart of tobacco smoke, one edge is squeezed out. Frog's heart—as they say in Russian Gulch. And Jingle Bells! I can only hope that my good old partners, replete with full houses and straights, will think I am bluffing.

VLADIMIR NABOKOV
March 28, 1967
Montreux

KING,
QUEEN,
KNAVE

1

The huge black clock hand is still at rest but is on the point of making its once-a-minute gesture; that resilient jolt will set a whole world in motion. The clock face will slowly turn away, full of despair, contempt, and boredom, as one by one the iron pillars will start walking past, bearing away the vault of the station like bland atlantes; the platform will begin to move past, carrying off on an unknown journey cigarette butts, used tickets, flecks of sunlight and spittle; a luggage handcart will glide by, its wheels motionless; it will be followed by a news stall hung with seductive magazine covers—photographs of naked, pearl-gray beauties; and people, people, people on the moving platform, themselves moving their feet, yet standing still, striding forward, yet retreating as in an agonizing dream full of incredible effort, nausea, a cottony weakness in one's calves, will surge back, almost falling supine.

There were more women than men as is always the case at partings. Franz's sister, with the pallor of the early hour on her thin cheeks, and an unpleasant, empty-stomach smell, dressed in a checked cape that surely one would never see on a city girl; and his mother, small, round, all in brown like a compact little monk. See the handkerchiefs beginning to flutter.

And not only did they slip away, those two familiar smiles; not only did the station depart removing its newsstand, its luggage cart, and a sandwich-and-fruit vendor with such nice, plump, lumpy, glossy red strawberries positively crying to be bitten into, all their achenes proclaiming their affinity with one's own tongue's papillae—but alas gone now; not only did all this fall behind; the entire old burg in its rosy autumn morning mist moved as well: the great stone *Herzog* in the square, the dark cathedral, the shop signs— top hat, a fish, the copper basin of a barber. There was no stopping the world now. In grand style houses pass by, the curtains flap in the open windows of his home, its floors crackle a little, the walls creak, his mother and sister are drinking their morning coffee in the swift draft, the furniture shudders from the quickening jolts, and ever more rapidly, more mysteriously, travel the houses, the cathedral, the square, the sidestreets. And even though by now tilled fields had long been unfolding their patchwork past the railway car window, Franz still felt in his very bones the receding motion of the townlet where he had lived for twenty years. Besides Franz, the wooden-benched third-class compartment contained two old ladies in corduroy dresses; a plump inevitably red-cheeked woman with the inevitable basket of eggs in her lap; and a blond youth in tan shorts, sturdy and angular, very much like his own rucksack, which was tightly stuffed and looked as if it had been hewed of yellow stone: this he had energetically shaken off and heaved onto the shelf. The seat by the door, opposite Franz, was occupied by a magazine with the picture of a breathtaking girl; and at a window in the corridor, his back to the compartment, stood a broad-shouldered man in a black overcoat.

[2]

The train was now going fast. Franz suddenly clutched his side, transfixed by the thought that he had lost his wallet which contained so much: the solid little ticket, and a stranger's visiting card with a precious address, and an inviolate month of human life in reichsmarks. The wallet was there all right, firm and warm. The old ladies began to stir and rustle, unwrapping sandwiches. The man in the corridor turned and, with a slight lurch, retreating half a step, and then overcoming the sway of the floor, entered the compartment.

Most of the nose had gone or had never grown. To what remained of its bridge the pale parchment-like skin adhered with a sickening tightness; the nostrils had lost all sense of decency and faced the flinching spectator like two sudden holes, black and asymmetrical; the cheeks and forehead showed a geographical range of shades—yellowish, pinkish, and very glossy. Had he inherited that mask? And if not, what illness, what explosion, what acid had disfigured him? He had practically no lips; the absence of eyelashes lent his blue eyes a startled expression. And yet the man was smartly dressed, well groomed and well built. He wore a double-breasted suit under his heavy overcoat. His hair was as sleek as a wig. He pulled up the knees of his trousers as he sat down with a leisurely movement, his gray-gloved hands opened the magazine he had left on the seat.

The shudder that had passed between Franz's shoulder blades now tapered to a strange sensation in his mouth. His tongue felt repulsively alive; his palate nastily moist. His memory opened its gallery of waxworks, and he knew, he knew that there, at its far end somewhere a chamber of horrors awaited him. He remembered a dog that had vomited on the threshold of a butcher's shop. He remembered a child, a mere toddler, who, bending with the difficulty of its age, had laboriously picked up and put to its lips a filthy thing resembling a baby's pacifier. He remembered an old man with a cough in a streetcar who had fired a clot of mucus into the ticket collector's hand. These were images that Franz usually held at bay but that always kept swarming in the background of his life greeting with a hysterical spasm any new impression that was kin to them. After a shock of that sort in those still recent days he would throw himself prone on his bed and try to fight off the fit of nausea. His recollections of school seemed always to be dodging away from possible, impossible, contacts with the grubby, pimply, slippery skin of some companion or other pressing him to join in a game or eager to impart some spitterish secret.

The man was leafing through the magazine, and the combination of his face with its enticing cover was intolerably grotesque. The ruddy egg woman sat next to the monster, her sleepy shoulder touching him. The youth's rucksack rubbed against his slick sticker-mottled black valise. And worst of all, the old ladies ignoring their foul neighbor munched their sandwiches and sucked on fuzzy sections of orange, wrapping the peels in scraps of paper and popping them daintily under the seat. But when the man put down his magazine and, without taking off his gloves, himself began eating a bun with cheese, glancing around provokingly, Franz could stand it no longer. He rose quickly, he lifted like a martyr his pale face, shook loose and pulled down his humble suitcase, collected his raincoat and hat and, banging his suitcase awkwardly against the doorjamb, fled into the corridor.

This particular coach had been hooked on to the express at a recent station, and the air in it was still fresh. He immediately felt a sense of relief. But the dizziness had not quite passed. A wall of beech trees was flickering by the window in a speckled sequence of sun and shade. He began tentatively to walk along the corridor clutching at knobs and things, and peering into the compartments. Only one had a free seat; he hesitated and went on, shaking off the image of two pasty-faced children with dust-black hands, their shoulders hunched up in expectation of a blow from their mother right on the nape as they quietly kept sliding off the seat to play among greasy scraps of papers on the unmentionable floor at the passengers' feet. Franz reached the end of the car and paused, struck by an extraordinary thought. This thought was so sweet, so audacious and exciting, that he had to take off his glasses and wipe them. "No, I can't, out of the question," said Franz under his breath, already realizing, however, that he could not conquer the temptation. Then checking the knot of his tie with thumb and forefinger, he crossed in a burst of clangor the unsteady connecting plates, and with an exquisite sinking feeling in the pit of his stomach passed into the next car.

It was a second-class schnellzug car, and to Franz second-class was something brightly attractive, even slightly sinful, smacking of spicy extravagance like a sip of thick white liqueur or that enormous grapefruit resembling a yellow skull that he had once bought on the way to school. About first-class one could not dream at all—that was for diplomats, generals, and almost unearthly actresses! Second, though . . . second. . . . If he could only get up the courage. They said his late father (a seedy notary) had on occasion—long ago, before the war—travelled second-class. Yet, Franz could not make up his mind. He stopped at the beginning of the corridor, by the placard listing the car inventory, and now it was no longer a fence-like forest glancing by but vast meadows majestically gliding past, and, in the distance, parallel to the tracks, flowed a highway, along which sped lickety-split a lilliputian automobile.

The conductor just then making his rounds brought him out of his difficulty. Franz bought a supplement promoting his ticket to the next rank. A short tunnel deafened him with its resounding darkness. Then it was light again but the conductor had vanished.

The compartment that Franz entered with a silent un-acknowledged bow was occupied by only two people—a handsome bright-eyed lady and a middle-aged man with a clipped tawny mustache. Franz hung up his raincoat and sat down carefully. The seat was so soft; there was such a cosy semi-circular projection at temple level separating one seat from the next; the photographs on the wall were so romantic —a flock of sheep, a cross on a rock, a waterfall. He slowly stretched out his long feet, slowly took a folded newspaper from his pocket. But he was unable to read. Benumbed with luxury he merely held the newspaper open and from behind it examined his fellow travellers. Oh, they were charming. The lady wore a black suit and a diminutive black hat with a little diamond swallow. Her face was serious, her eyes cold, a little dark down, the sign of passion, glistened above her upper lip, and a gleam of sun brought out the creamy tex-ture of her neck at the throat with its two delicate transverse lines as if traced with a fingernail across it, one above the other: also a token of all kinds of marvels, according to one of his schoolmates, a precocious expert. The man must be a foreigner, judging by his soft collar and tweeds. Franz, how-ever, was mistaken.

"I'm thirsty," said the man with a Berlin accent. "Too bad there's no fruit. Those strawberries were positively dying to be sampled."

"It's your own fault," answered the lady in a displeased

voice, adding a little later: "I still cannot get over it—it was such a silly thing to do."

Dreyer briefly cast up his eyes to a makeshift heaven and made no reply.

"It's your own fault," she repeated and automatically pulled at her pleated skirt, automatically noticing that the awkward young man with the glasses who had appeared in the door corner seemed to be fascinated by the sheer silk of her legs.

"Anyway," she said, "it's not worth discussing."

Dreyer knew that his silence irritated Martha unspeakably. There was a boyish gleam in his eye, and the soft folds about his lips were undulating because he was rolling a mint in his mouth. The incident that had irritated his wife was actually pretty silly. They had spent August and half of September in Tyrol, and now, on the way home, had stopped for a few days on business in that quaint little town, and there he had called on his cousin Lina with whom he had danced in his youth, some twenty-five years ago. His wife had flatly refused to accompany him. Lina, now a roly-poly creature with false teeth but just as talkative and amiable as ever, found that the years had left their mark on him but that it might have been worse; she served him excellent coffee, told him about her children, said she was sorry they were not at home, asked about Martha (whom she did not know) and his business (about which she was well informed); then, after a pious pause, she wondered if he could give her a piece of advice. . . .

It was warm in the room where around the aged chandelier, with gray little glass pendants like dirty icicles, flies were describing parallelograms, lighting every time on the same pendants (which for some reason amused him), and the old chairs extended their plush-covered arms with comical cordiality. An old pug dozed on an embroidered cushion. In reply to the expectant interrogatory sigh of his cousin he had suddenly said, coming to life with a laugh: "Well, why don't you have him come to see me in Berlin? I'll give him a job." And that was what his wife could not forgive him. She called it "swamping the business with poor relations"; but when you come down to it, how can one poor relation swamp anything? Knowing that Lina would invite his wife, and that Martha would not go in any circumstance, he had lied, telling his cousin that they were leaving the same evening. Instead, Martha and he had visited a fair and the splendid vineyards of a business friend. A week later at the station, when they had already settled down in their compartment, he had glimpsed Lina from the window. It was a wonder they had not run into her somewhere in town. Martha wanted to avoid her seeing them at all cost, and even though the idea of buying a nest of fruit for the trip appealed to him greatly he did not put his head out of the window, did not beckon with a soft "psst" the young vendor in the white jacket.

Comfortably dressed, in perfect health, a colored mist of vague pleasant thoughts in his head and a peppermint in his mouth, Dreyer sat with crossed arms, and the soft folds of the fabric in the crook of his arms matched the soft folds of his cheeks, and the outline of his clipped mustache, and the wrinkles fanning templeward from his eyes. With a peculiar blandly amused gleam in his eyes he gazed from under his brows at the green landscape gliding in the window, at Martha's handsome profile rimmed with sunlight, and the cheap suitcase of the bespectacled young man who was reading a newspaper in the corner by the door. Idly he considered that passenger, palpating him from all sides. He noted the so-called "lizard" pattern of the young fellow's green-and-garnet tie which obviously had cost ninety-five pfennigs, the stiff collar, and also the cuffs and front of his shirt—a shirt incidentally which only existed in an abstract form since all its visible parts, judging by a treacherous gloss, were pieces of starched armor of rather low quality but greatly esteemed by a frugal provincial who attaches them to an invisible undergarment made at home of unbleached cloth. As to the young man's suit, it evoked a delicate melancholy in Dreyer as he reflected not for the first time on the pathetically short life of every new cut: that kind of three-button, narrow-lapelled blue jacket with a pin stripe had disappeared from most Berlin stores at least five years ago.

Two alarmed eyes were suddenly born in the lenses, and Dreyer turned away. Martha said:

"It is all so silly. I wish you had listened to me."

Her husband sighed and said nothing. She wanted to go on—there were still lots of pithy rebukes she could make but she felt the young man was listening and, instead of words, leaned her elbow abruptly on the window side of the table leaf—pulling up the skin of her cheek with her knuckles. She sat that way until the flicker of woods in the window became irksome; she slowly straightened her ripe body, annoyed and bored, then leaned back and closed her eyes. The sun penetrated her eyelids with solid scarlet, across which luminous stripes moved in succession (the ghostly negative of the passing forest), and a replica of her husband's cheerful face, as if slowly rotating toward her, got mixed up in this barred redness, and she opened her eyes with a start. Her husband, however, was sitting relatively far, reading a book bound in purple morocco. He was reading attentively and with pleasure. Nothing existed beyond the sunlit page. He turned the page, looked around, and the outside world avidly, like a playful dog waiting for that moment, darted up to him with a bright bound. But pushing Tom away affectionately, Dreyer again immersed himself in his anthology of verse.

For Martha that frolicsome radiance was simply the stuffy air in a swaying railway car. It is supposed to be stuffy in a car: that is customary and therefore good. Life should proceed according to plan, straight and strict, without freakish twists and wiggles. An elegant book is all right on a drawing-room table. In a railway car, to allay boredom, one can leaf through some trashy magazine. But to imbibe and relish . . . poems, if you please . . . in an expensive binding . . . a person who calls himself a businessman cannot, must not, dare not act like that. But for that matter, perhaps, he may be doing it on purpose, to spite me. Just another of his show-off whims. Very well, my friend, keep showing off. How nice it would be to pluck that book out of his hands and lock it up in a suitcase.

At that instant the sun seemed to lay bare her face, flowing over her smooth cheeks and lending an artificial warmth to her eyes with their large elastic-looking pupils amid the dove-gray iris and adorable dark lids slightly creased like violets, radiantly lashed and rarely blinking as if she were constantly afraid of losing sight of an essential goal. She wore almost no make-up—only in the minute transverse fissures of her full lips there seemed to be drying traces of orange-red paint.

Franz, who had been hiding behind his newspaper in a state of blissful nonexistence, living on the outside of himself, in the chance motions and chance words of his travelling companions, now started to assert himself and openly, almost arrogantly, looked at the lady.

Yet only a moment ago his thoughts always tending to morbid associations had blended, in one of those falsely harmonious images that are significant within the dream but meaningless when one recalls it, two recent events. The transition from the third-class compartment, where a nose-less monster reigned in silence, into this sunny plush room appeared to him like the passage from a hideous hell through the purgatory of the corridors and intervestibular clatter into a little abode of bliss. The old conductor who had punched his ticket a short while ago and promptly vanished might have been as humble and omnipotent as St. Peter. Pious popular prints that had frightened him in child-hood came to life again. He transformed the conductor's click into that of a key unlocking the gates of paradise. So a grease-painted gaudy-faced actor in a miracle play passes across a long stage divided into three parts, from the jaws of the devil into the shelter of angels. And Franz, in order to drive away the old obsessive fantasy, eagerly started to seek human, everyday tokens that would break the spell.

Martha helped him. While looking sideways out of the window she yawned: he glimpsed the swell of her tense tongue in the red penumbra of her mouth and the flash of her teeth before her hand shot up to her mouth to stop her soul from escaping; whereupon she blinked, dispersing a tickling tear with the beat of her eyelashes. Franz was not one to resist the example of a yawn, especially one that re-sembled somehow those luscious lascivious autumn straw-berries for which his hometown was famous. At the moment when, unable to overcome the force prying his palate, he convulsively opened his mouth, Martha happened to glance at him, and he realized, snarling and weeping, that she real-ized he had been looking at her. The morbid bliss he had shortly before experienced as he looked at her dissolving face now turned into acute embarrassment. He knit his brows under her radiant and indifferent gaze and, when she turned away, mentally calculated, as though his fingers had rattled across the counters of a secret abacus, how many days of his life he would give to possess this woman.

The door slid open, and an excited waiter, the herald of some frightful disaster, thrust his head in, barked his message, and dashed on to the next compartment to cry his news.

Basically Martha was opposed to those fraudulent frivolous meals, with the railway company charging you exorbitant prices for mediocre food, and this almost physical sensation of needless expense, mixed with the feeling that someone, snug and robust, wanted to cheat her proved to be so strong that were it not for a ravenous hunger she would certainly not have gone that long vacillating way to the dining car. She vaguely envied the bespectacled young man who reached into the pocket of his raincoat hanging beside him and pulled out a sandwich. She got up and took her handbag under her arm. Dreyer found the violet ribbon in his book, marked his page with it, and after waiting a couple of seconds as if he could not immediately make the transition from one world to the other, gave his knees a light slap and stood up too. He instantly filled the whole compartment, being one of those men who despite medium height and moderate corpulence create an impression of extraordinary bulk. Franz retracted his feet. Martha and her husband lurched past him and went out.

He was left alone with his gray sandwich in the now spacious compartment. He munched and gazed out of the window. A green bank was rising there diagonally until it suffused the window to the top. Then, resolving an iron chord, a bridge banged overhead and instantly the green slope vanished and open country unfurled—fields, willows, a golden birch tree, a winding brook, beds of cabbage. Franz finished his sandwich, fidgeted cozily, and closed his eyes.

Berlin! In that very name of the still unfamiliar metropolis, in the lumber and rumble of the first syllable and in the light ring of the second there was something that excited him like the romantic names of good wines and bad women. The express seemed already to be speeding along the famous avenue lined for him with gigantic ancient lindens beneath which seethed for him a flamboyant crowd. The express sped past those lindens grown so luxuriantly out of the avenue's resonant name, and ("derlin, derlin" went the bell of the waiter summoning belated diners) shot under an enormous arch ornamented with mother-of-pearl spangles. Farther on there was an enchanting mist where another picture postcard turned on its stand showing a translucent tower against a black background. It vanished, and, in a brilliantly lit-up emporium, among gilded dummies, limpid mirrors, and glass counters, Franz strolled about in cut-away, striped trousers, and white spats, and with a smooth movement of his hand directed customers to the departments they needed. This was no longer a wholly conscious play of thought, nor was it yet a dream; and at the instant that sleep was about to trip him up, Franz regained control of himself and directed his thoughts according to his wishes. He promised himself a lone treat that very night. He bared the shoulders of the woman that had just been sitting by the window, made a quick mental test (did blind Eros react? clumsy Eros did, unsticking its folds in the dark); then, keeping the splendid shoulders, changed the head, substituting for it the face of that seventeen-year-old maid who had vanished with a silver soup ladle almost as big as she before he had had time to declare his love; but that head too he erased and, in its

[13]

place, attached the face of one of those bold-eyed, humid-lipped Berlin beauties that one encounters mainly in liquor and cigarette advertisements. Only then did the image come to life: the bare-bosomed girl lifted a wine glass to her crimson lips, gently swinging her apricot-silk leg as a red backless slipper slowly slid off her foot. The slipper fell off, and Franz, bending down after it, plunged softly into dark slumber. He slept with mouth agape so that his pale face presented three apertures, two shiny ones (his glasses) and one black (his mouth). Dreyer noticed this symmetry when an hour later he returned with Martha from the dining car. In silence they stepped over a lifeless leg. Martha put her handbag on the collapsible window table, and the bag's nickel clasp with its cat's eye immediately came to life as a green reflection began dancing in it. Dreyer took out a cigar but did not light it.

The dinner, particularly that wiener schnitzel, had turned out to be pretty good, and Martha was not sorry now that she had agreed to go. Her complexion had grown warmer, her exquisite eyes were moist, her freshly painted lips glistened. She smiled, only just baring her incisors, and this contented, precious smile lingered on her face for several instants. Dreyer lazily admired her, his eyes slightly narrowed, savoring her smile as one might an unexpected gift, but nothing on earth could have made him show that pleasure. When the smile disappeared he turned away as a satisfied gawker drifts away after the bicyclist has picked himself up, and the street vendor has replaced on his cart the scattered fruit.

Franz crossed his legs like one very lame and slow but did not wake up. Harshly the train began braking. There glided past a brick wall, an enormous chimney, freight cars standing on a siding. Presently it grew dark in the compartment: they had entered a vast domed station.

"I'll go out, my love," said Dreyer, who liked to smoke in the open air.

Left alone, Martha leaned back in the corner, and having nothing better to do looked at the bespectacled corpse in the corner, thinking indifferently that this, perhaps, was the young man's stop and he would miss it. Dreyer strode along the platform, drummed with five fingers on the windowpane as he passed, but his wife did not smile again. With a puff of smoke he moved on. He strolled leisurely, with a bouncing gait, his hands clasped behind his back, and his cigar thrust forward. He reflected that it would be nice some day to be promenading like this beneath the glazed arches of a remote station somewhere on the way to Andalusia, Bagdad or Nizhni Novgorod. Actually one could set off any time; the globe was enormous and round, and he had enough spare cash to circle it completely half-a-dozen times. Martha, though, would refuse to come, preferring a trim suburban lawn to the most luxuriant jungle. She would only sniff sarcastically were he to suggest they take a year off. "I suppose," he thought, "I ought to buy a paper. I guess the stock market is also an interesting and tricky subject. And let us see if our two aviators—or is it some wonderful hoax?—have managed to duplicate in reverse direction that young American's feat of four months ago. America, Mexico, Palm Beach. Willy Wald was there, wanted us to accompany him. No, there is no breaking her down. Now then, where is the newsstand? That old sewing machine with its arthritic pedal wrapped up in brown paper is so clear right now, and yet in an hour or two I shall forget it forever; I shall forget that I looked at it; I shall forget everything. . . ." Just then a whistle blew, and the baggage car moved. Hey, that's my train! Dreyer made for the newsstand at a smart trot, selected a coin from his palm, snatched the paper he wanted, dropped it, retrieved it, and dashed back. Not very gracefully, he hopped onto a passing step, and could not open the door immediately. In the struggle he lost his cigar but not his paper. Chuckling and panting, he walked through one car, another, a third. In the next to last corridor a big fellow in a black overcoat who was pulling a window shut moved to let him by. Glancing at him as he passed, Dreyer saw the grinning face of a grown man with the nose of a baby monkey. "Curious," thought Dreyer; "ought to get such a dummy to display something funny." In the next car he found his compartment, stepped across the lifeless leg, by now a familiar fixture, and quietly sat down. Martha was apparently asleep. He opened the paper, and then noticed that her eyes were fixed upon him.

"Crazy idiot," she said calmly and closed her eyes again. Dreyer nodded amiably and immersed himself in his paper.

The first chapter of a journey is always detailed and slow. Its middle hours are drowsy, and the last ones swift. Presently Franz awoke and made some chewing motions with his lips. His travelling companions were sleeping. The light in the window had dimmed, but in compensation the reflection of Martha's little bright swallow had appeared in it. Franz glanced at his wrist, at the watch face sturdily protected by its metal mesh. A lot of time, however, had escaped from that prison cell. There was a most repulsive taste in his mouth. He carefully wiped with a special square of cloth his glasses, and made his way out into the corridor in search of the toilet. As he stood there holding on to an iron handle, he found it strange and dreadful to be connected to a cold hole quite ready to give you my permission but there is my wife, you see—she happens to be away temporarily—but I know she would never allow such visits."

Franz flushed and hastily nodded in assent. His landlord's assumption flattered and excited him. He imagined her fragrant, warm-looking lips, her creamy skin, but cut short the habitual swell of desire. "She is not for me," he thought glumly, "she is remote and cold. She lives in a different world, with a very rich and still vigorous husband. She'd send me packing if I were to grow enterprising; my career would be ruined." On the other hand, he thought he might find himself a sweetheart anyway. She too would be shapely, sleek, ripe-lipped and dark-haired. And with this in mind he decided to take certain measures. In the morning, when the landlord brought him his coffee, Franz cleared his throat and said: "Listen, if I paid you a small supplement, would you. . . . Would I. . . . What I mean is, could I entertain anyone if I wished?"

"That depends," said the old man.

"A few extra marks," said Franz.

"I understand," said the old man.

"Five marks more per month," said Franz.

"That's generous," said the old man, and as he turned to go added in a sly admonitory tone: "But take care not to be late for work."

Thus Martha's haggling had all been for nought. Having resolved to pay the extra sum secretly, Franz knew perfectly well he had acted rashly. His money was melting away, and still Dreyer did not telephone. For four days running he left the house in disgust punctually at eight, returning at nightfall in a fog of fatigue. He was completely fed up by now with the celebrated avenue. He sent a postcard to his mother with a view of the Brandenburg Gate, and wrote that he was well, and that Dreyer was a very kind uncle. There was no use frightening her, though perhaps she deserved it. And only on Friday night, when Franz was already lying in bed and saying to himself with a tremor of panic that they had all forgotten him, that he was completely alone in a strange city, and thinking with a certain evil joy that he would stop being faithful to the radiant Martha presiding over his nightly surrenders and ask lewd old Enricht, his landlord, to let him have a bath in the grimy tub of the flat and direct him to the nearest brothel. At that instant Enricht in a sleepy voice called him to the telephone.

With terrible haste and excitement, Franz pulled on his pants and rushed barefoot into the passage. A trunk managed to bang him on the knee as he made for the gleam of the telephone at the end of the corridor. Owing perhaps to his being unaccustomed to telephones, he could not identify at first the voice barking in his ear. "Come to my house this minute," the voice said clearly at last. "Do you hear me? Please hurry, I am waiting for you."

"Oh, how are you, how are you?" Franz babbled, but the telephone was dead. Dreyer put down the receiver with a flourish and continued rapidly jotting down the things he had to do tomorrow. Then he glanced at his watch, reflecting that his wife would be back from the cinema any moment now. He rubbed his forehead, and then with a sly smile took from a drawer a bunch of keys, and a sausage-shaped flashlight with a convex eye. He still had his coat on, for he had just come home and without shedding it had strode right to his study as he always did when he was in a hurry to write something down or telephone someone. Now he noisily pushed back his chair, and began taking off his voluminous camel-hair coat as he walked to the front hall to hang it up there. Into its capacious pocket he dropped the keys and the flashlight. Tom, who was lying by the door, got up and rubbed his soft head against Dreyer's leg. Dreyer resonantly locked himself up in the bathroom where three or four senile mosquitoes slept on the whitewashed wall. A minute later, turning down and buttoning up his sleeves at the wrists, he proceeded with another leisurely homy gait toward the dining room.

The table was laid for two, and a dark red Westphalian ham reposed on a dish, amid a mosaic of sausage slices. Large grapes, brimming with greenish light, hung over the edge of their vase. Dreyer plucked off one and tossed it in his mouth. He cast a sidelong glance at the salami but decided to wait for Martha. The mirror reflected his broad back clothed in gray flannel and the tawny strands of his smoothly brushed hair. He turned around quickly as though feeling that someone was watching him, and moved away; all that remained in the mirror was a white corner of the table against the black background broken by a crystal glimmer on the sideboard. He heard a faint sound from the far side of that stillness: a little key was seeking a sensitive point in the stillness; it found and pierced that point, and gave one crisp turn, and then everything came to life. Dreyer's gray shoulder passed and repassed in the mirror as he paced hungrily round the table. The front door slammed and in came Martha. Her eyes glistened, she was wiping her nose firmly with a Chanel-scented handkerchief. Behind her came the fully awakened dog.

"Sit down, sit down, my love," said Dreyer briskly, and turned on the sophisticated electric current to warm the tea water.

"Lovely film," she said. "Hess was wonderful, though I think I liked him better in *The Prince*."

"In what?"

"Oh you remember, the student at Heidelberg disguised as a Hindu prince."

Martha was smiling. In fact, she smiled fairly often of late, which gladdened Dreyer ineffably. She was in the pleasant position of a person who has been promised a mysterious treat in the near future. She was willing to wait awhile, knowing that the treat would come without fail. That day she had summoned the painters to have them brighten up the south side of the terrace wall. A banquet scene in the film had made her hungry, and now she intended to betray her diet, then roll into bed, and perhaps allow Dreyer his long-deferred due.

The front-door bell tinkled. Tom barked briskly. Martha raised her thin eyebrows in surprise. Dreyer got up with a chuckle, and, chewing as he went, marched into the front hall.

She sat half-turned toward the door, holding her raised cup. When Franz, jokingly nudged on by Dreyer, stepped into the dining room, clicked his heels, and quickly walked up to her, she beamed so beautifully, her lips glistened so warmly that within Dreyer's soul a huge merry throng seemed to break out in deafening applause, and he thought that after a smile like that everything was bound to go well: Martha, as she once used to, would tell him in breathless detail the entire foolish film as the preface and price of a submissive caress; and on Sunday, instead of tennis, he would go riding with her in the rustling, sun-flecked, orange-and-red park.

"First of all, my dear Franz," he said, drawing up a chair for his nephew, "have a bite of something. And here is a drop of kirsch for you."

Like an automaton, Franz stuck out his hand across the table, aiming for the proffered snifter, and knocked over a slender vase enclosing a heavy brown rose ("Which should have been removed long ago," reflected Martha). The liberated water spread across the tablecloth.

He lost his composure, and no wonder. In the first place, he had not expected to see Martha. Secondly, he had thought Dreyer would receive him in his study and inform him about a very, very important job that had to be tackled immediately. Martha's smile had stunned him. He ascertained to himself the reason for his alarm. Like the fake seed a fakir buries in the ground only to draw out of it at once, with manic magic, a live rose tree, Martha's request that he conceal from Dreyer their innocent adventure—a request to which he had barely paid attention at the time—now, in the husband's presence had fabulously swelled, turning into a secret erotic bond. He also remembered old Enricht's words about a lady friend, and those words confirmed as it were the bliss and the shame. He tried to cast off the spell— but, meeting her unbearably intense gaze, dropped his eyes and helplessly continued to dab the wet tablecloth with his handkerchief despite Dreyer's trying to push his hand away. Moments ago he had been lying in bed and now here he sat, in this resplendent dining room, suffering as if in a dream because he could not halt the dark streamlet that had rounded the saltcellar, and under cover of the plate's rim was endeavoring to reach the edge of the table. Still smiling (the tablecloth would have to be changed tomorrow anyway), Martha shifted her gaze to his hands, to the gentle play of the knuckles under the taut skin, to the hairy wrist, to the long groping fingers, and felt oddly aware she had nothing woollen on her body that night.

Abruptly Dreyer got up and said: "Franz, this is not very hospitable, but it can't be helped. It's getting late, and you and I must be on our way."

"On our way?" Franz uttered in confusion, thrusting the wet ball of his handkerchief into his pocket. Martha glanced at her husband with cold surprise.

"You'll understand presently," said Dreyer, his eyes twinkling with an adventurous light that was all too familiar to Martha. "What a bore," she thought angrily, "what is he up to?"

She stopped him for a moment in the front hall and asked him in rapid whisper: "Where are you going, where are you going? I demand to be told where you are going."

"On a wild spree," replied Dreyer, hoping to provoke another marvellous smile.

She winced in disgust. He patted her on the cheek and went out.

Martha wandered back to the dining room and stood lost in thought behind the chair Franz had vacated. Then with irritation she lifted the tablecloth where the water had been spilled, and slipped a plate bottom up under it. The looking glass, which was working hard that night, reflected her green dress, her white neck under the dark weight of her chignon, and the gleam of her emerald earrings. She remained unconscious of the mirror's attention, and as she slowly went about putting the fruit knives away her reflection would reappear every now and then. Frieda joined her for a minute or two. Then the light in the dining room clicked off, and, nibbling at her necklace, Martha went upstairs to her bedroom.

"I bet he wants me to think he is kidding because he isn't. I bet it's exactly the way it will be," she thought. "He'll fix him up with some dirty slut. And that will be the end of it."

As she undressed, she felt she was about to cry. Just you wait, just you wait till you get home. Especially if you were pulling my leg. And what manners, what manners! You invite the poor boy and then whisk him away. In the middle of the night! Disgraceful!

Once again, as so many times previously, she went over all her husband's transgressions in her memory. It seemed to her that she remembered them all. They were numerous. That did not prevent her, however, from assuring her married sister Hilda, when the latter would come from Hamburg, that she was happy, that her marriage was a happy one.

And Martha really did believe that her marriage was no different from any other marriage, that discord always reigned, that the wife always struggled against her husband, against his peculiarities, against his departures from the accepted rules, and all this amounted to happy marriage. An unhappy marriage was when the husband was poor, or had landed in prison for some shady business, or kept squandering his earnings on kept women. Therefore Martha never complained about her situation, since it was a natural and customary one.

Her mother had died when Martha was three—a not unusual arrangement. A first stepmother soon died too, and that also ran in some families. The second and final stepmother, who died only recently, was a lovely woman of quite gentle birth whom everybody adored. Papa, who had started his career as a saddler and ended it as the bankrupt owner of an artificial leather factory, was desperately eager she marry the "Hussar," as for some reason he dubbed Dreyer, whom she barely knew when he proposed in 1920, at the same time that Hilda became engaged to the fat little purser of a second-rate Atlantic liner. Dreyer was getting rich with miraculous ease; he was fairly attractive, but bizarre and unpredictable; sang off-key silly arias and made her silly presents.

As a well-bred girl with long lashes and glowing cheeks, she said she would make up her mind the next time he came to Hamburg. Before leaving for Berlin he gave her a monkey which she loathed; fortunately, a handsome young cousin with whom she had gone rather far before he became one of Hilda's first lovers taught it to light matches, its little jersey caught fire, and the clumsy animal had to be destroyed. When Dreyer returned a week later, she allowed him to kiss her on the cheek. Poor old Papa got so high at the party that he beat up the fiddler, which was pardonable—seeing all the hard luck he had encountered in his long life. It was only after the wedding, when her husband cancelled an important business trip in favor of a ridiculous honeymoon in Norway—why Norway of all places?—that certain doubts began to assail her; but the villa in Grunewald soon dissipated them, and so on, not very interesting recollections.

4

In the darkness of the taxi (the unfortunate Icarus was still being repaired, and the rented substitute, a quirky Oriole, had not been a success), Dreyer remained mysteriously silent. He might have been asleep, had not his cigar glowed rhythmically. Franz was silent too, wondering uneasily where he was being taken. After the third or fourth turn he lost all sense of direction.

Up to now he had explored, besides the quiet quarter where he lived, only the avenue of lindens and its surroundings at the other end of the city. Everything that lay between those two live oases was a *terra incognita* blank. He gazed out of the window and saw the dark streets gradually acquiring a certain limpidity, then dimming again, then again welling with light, waning once more, brightening again, until having matured in the darkness they suddenly burst forth scintillating with fabulous colors, gemmed cascades, blazing advertisements. A tall steepled church glided past under the umber sky. Presently, skidding slightly on the damp asphalt, the car drew up at the curb.

Only then did Franz understand. In sapphire letters with a diamond flourish prolonging the final vowel, a glittering forty-foot sign spelled the word D*A*N*D*Y—which now he remembered hearing before, the fool that he was! Dreyer took him under the arm and led him up to one of the ten radiantly lit display windows. Like tropical blossoms in a hothouse, ties and socks vied in delicate shades with the rectangles of folded shirts or drooped lazily from gilded bows, while in the depths an opal-tinted pajama with the face of an Oriental idol stood fully erect, god of that garden. But Dreyer did not allow Franz to dally in contemplation. He led him smartly past the other windows, and there flashed by in turn an orgy of glossy footwear, a Fata Morgana of coats, a graceful flight of hats, gloves, and canes, and a sunny paradise of sports articles; then Franz found himself in a dark passageway where stood an old man in a black cape with a badge on his visored cap next to a slender-legged woman in furs. They both looked at Dreyer. The watchman recognized him and put his hand to his cap. The bright-eyed prostitute glanced at Franz and modestly moved away. As soon as he disappeared behind Dreyer in the gloom of a courtyard, she resumed her talk with the watchman about rheumatism and its cures.

The yard formed a triangular dead end between window-less walls. There was an odor of damp mingled with that of urine and beer. In one corner, either something was dumped, or else it was a cart with its shafts in the air. Dreyer produced the flashlight from his pocket, and a skimming circle of gray light outlined a grating, the moving shadows of descending steps, an iron door. Taking a childish delight in choosing the most mysterious entrance, Dreyer unlocked the door. Franz ducked and followed him into a dark stone passage where the round of flitting light now picked out a door. If any illegal attempt had been made to tamper with it, it would have emitted a wild ringing. But for this door too Dreyer had a small noiseless key, and again Franz ducked. In the murky basement through which they walked one could distinguish sacks and crates piled here and there and something like straw rustled underfoot. The mobile beam turned a corner, and yet another door appeared. Beyond it rose a bare staircase that melted into the blackness. They shuffled up the stone steps, explorers of a buried temple. With dream-like unexpectedness they emerged presently into a vast hall. The light glanced across metallic gallows, then along folds of drapery, gigantic wardrobes, swinging mirrors and broad-shouldered black figures. Dreyer stopped, put away his light and said softly in the dark "Attention!" His hand could be heard fumbling, and a single pear-shaped bulb brightly illuminated a counter. The remainder of the hall—an endless labyrinth—remained submerged in darkness, and Franz found it a little eerie to have this one nook singled out by the strong light. "Lesson One," Dreyer said solemnly, and with a flourish went behind the counter.

It is doubtful if Franz benefited from this fantastic night lesson—everything was too strange, and Dreyer impersonated a salesman with too much whimsy. And yet, despite the baroque nonsense there was something about the angular reflections and the surrounding spectral abyss, where vague fabrics that had been handled and re-handled during the day reposed in weary attitudes, which long remained in Franz's memory and imparted a certain dark luxurious coloring, at least at first, to the basic background against which his everyday salesman's toil began to sketch later its plain, comprehensible, often tiresome pattern. And it was not on personal experience, not on the recollection of distant days when he actually had worked behind the counter, that Dreyer drew that night as he showed Franz how to sell

neckties. Instead, he soared into the ravishing realm of
inutile imagination, demonstrating not the way ties should
be sold in real life, but the way they might be sold if the
salesman were both artist and clairvoyant.

"I want a simple blue one," Franz, prompted by him,
would say in a wooden schoolboy voice.

"Certainly, sir," Dreyer answered briskly and, whisking off
several cardboard boxes from a shelf, nimbly opened them
on the counter.

"How do you like this one?" he inquired not without a
shadow of pensiveness, knotting a mottled magenta-and-
black tie on his hand and holding it away a little as if admir-
ing it himself in the capacity of an independent artist.

Franz was silent.

"An important technique," explained Dreyer, changing his
voice. "Let's see if you got the point. Now you go behind the
counter. In this box here there are some solid-colored ties.
They cost four-five marks. And here we have stylish ones on
the "orchid" side, as we say, at eight, ten, or even fourteen,
the Lord forgive us. Now then, you are the salesman and I
am a young man, a ninny if you'll excuse me—inexperi-
enced, irresolute, easily tempted."

Franz self-consciously went behind the counter. Hunching
his shoulders and narrowing his eyes as if he were near-
sighted, Dreyer said in a high-pitched quaver: "I want a
plain blue one. . . . And please, not too expensive." "Smile,"
he added in a prompter's whisper.

Franz bent low over one of the boxes, fumbled awkwardly
and produced a plain blue tie.

"Aha, I caught you!" Dreyer exclaimed cheerfully. "I
knew you had not understood, or else you are color-blind,
and then good-by dear uncle and aunt. Why on earth must
you give me the cheapest one? You should have done as I

did—stun the ninny first with an expensive one, no matter what color. But be sure it's gaudy and costly, or costly and elegant, and maybe squeeze out of him 'an extra throb and an extra bob,' as they say in London. Here, take this one. Now knot it on your hand. Wait, wait—don't worry it like that. Swing it around your finger. Thus! Remember the slightest delay in the rhythm costs you a moment of the customer's attention. Hypnotize him with the flip of the tie you display. You must make it *bloom* before the idiot's eyes. No, that's not a knot, that's some kind of tumor. Watch. Hold your hand straight. Let's try this expensive vampire red. Now we suppose it is I who am looking at it, and I still don't yield to temptation."

"But I wanted a plain blue one," said Dreyer in a high voice—and then, again in a whisper: "Ah, no—keep pushing the vampire one in his stupid face, perhaps you'll wear him down. And watch him, watch his eyes—if he looks at the thing that's already something. Only if he does not look at all and begins to frown, and clear his damned throat—only then, you understand, only then give him what he requested—always choosing the dearest of the three plain blues, of course. But even as you yield to his coarse request, give, you know, a slight shrug, look at me now—and smile sort of disdainfully as if to say 'this isn't fashionable at all, frankly, this is for peasants, for droshky coachmen . . . but if you really want it'—"

"I'll take this blue one," said Dreyer in his comedy voice.

Franz grimly handed him the tie across the counter. Dreyer's guffaw awakened a rude echo. "No," he said, "no, my friend. Not at all. First, you lay it aside to your right, then you inquire if he does not need something else, for instance, handkerchiefs, or some fancy studs, and only after he has thought a bit and shaken his calf's head, only then produce this fountain pen (which is a present) and write out and give him the price slip for the cashier. But the rest is routine. No, keep it, I said. You will be shown that part tomorrow by Mr. Piffke, a very pedantic man. Now let's continue."

Dreyer hoisted himself a little heavily to a sitting position on the counter, casting as he did so a sharp black shadow that dived head first into the darkness which seemed to have moved closer the better to hear. He started to finger the silks in the boxes, and to instruct Franz how to remember ties by touch and tint, how to develop, in other words (lost on Franz), a chromatic and tactile memory, how to eradicate from one's artistic and commercial consciousness styles and specimens that had been sold out—so as to make room for new ones in one's mind, and how to determine the price in marks immediately and then add the pfennigs from the tag. Several times he jumped off the counter, gesticulating grotesquely, impersonating a customer irritated by everything he was shown; the brute who objected to his being told the price before he had asked for it; and the saint to whom price was no object; also an old lady buying a tie for her grandson, a fireman at Potsdam; or a foreigner unable to express anything comprehensible—a Frenchman who wants a *cravate*, an Italian who demands a *cravatta*, a Russian who pleads gently for a *galstook*. Whereupon he would reply at once to himself, pressing his fingers lightly against the counter, and for each occasion inventing a particular variety of intonation and smile. Then seating himself again and slightly swinging his foot in its glossy shoe (as his shadow flapped a black wing on the floor), he discussed the tender and cheerful attitude a salesman should have toward man-made things, and he confessed that sometimes one felt absurdly sorry for outmoded ties and obsolete socks that were still so neat and fresh but completely unwanted; an odd, dreamy smile hovered under his mustache, and alternately creased and smoothed out the wrinkles at the corners of his eyes and mouth—whilst extenuated Franz, leaning against a wardrobe, listened in a torpor to him.

Dreyer paused—and as Franz realized that the lesson was over, he could not help casting a covetous glance at the iridescent wonders now scattered, in real life, on the counter. Again producing his flashlight and turning off the switch on the wall, Dreyer led Franz over a waste of dark carpeting into the shadowy depths of the hall. He flung off in passing the canvas of a small table and trained his light on cuff links sparkling like eyes on their blue velvet cushion. A little further with playful nonchalance he tipped off its stand a huge beach ball which rolled soundlessly away into the dark, far, far, all the way to the Bay of Pomerania and its soft white sands.

They walked back along the stone passages, and as he was locking the last door Dreyer recalled not without pleasure the enigmatic disorder he had left behind while neglecting to think that perhaps someone else would be held responsible for it.

As soon as they emerged from the dark courtyard into the wetly gleaming street, Dreyer hailed a passing taxi and offered Franz a lift home.

Franz hesitated, staring at the festive vista (at last!) of the animated boulevard.

"Or do you have a date with a" (Dreyer consulted his wrist watch) "sleepy sweetheart?"

Franz licked his lips and shook his head.

"As you wish," said Dreyer with a laugh and, thrusting his head out of the cab, he shouted in parting: "Be at the store tomorrow, nine o'clock sharp."

The lustre of the black asphalt was filmed by a blend of dim hues, through which here and there vivid rends and oval holes made by rain puddles revealed the authentic colors of deep reflections—a vermilion diagonal band, a cobalt wedge, a green spiral—scattered glimpses into a humid upside-down world, into a dizzy geometry of gems. The kaleidoscopic effect suggested someone's jiggling every now and then the pavement so as to change the combination of numberless colored fragments. Meanwhile, shafts and ripples of life passed by, marking the course of every car. Shop windows, bursting with tense radiance, oozed, squirted, and splashed out into the rich blackness.

And at every corner, emblem of ineffable happiness, stood a sleek-hosed harlot whose features there was no time to study: another already beckoned in the distance, and beyond her, a third. And Franz knew without any doubt where those mysterious live beacons led. Every street lamp, its halo spreading like a spiky star, every rosy glow, every spasm of golden light, and the silhouettes of lovers pulsating against each other in every recess of porch and passage; and those half-opened painted lips that fleeted past him; and the black, moist, tender asphalt—all of it was assuming a specific significance and finding a name.

Saturated with sweat, limp with delicious languor, moving with the slow motion of a sleepwalker called back to his rumpled warm pillow, Franz went back to bed, without having noticed how he had re-entered the house and reached his room. He stretched, he passed his palms over his hairy legs, unglued and cupped himself, and almost instantly Sleep, with a bow, handed him the key of its city: he understood the meaning of all the lights, sounds, and perfumes as everything blended into a single blissful image. Now he seemed to be in a mirrored hall, which wondrously opened on a watery abyss, water glistened in the most unexpected places: he went toward a door past the perfectly credible motorcycle which his landlord was starting with his red heel, and, anticipating indescribable bliss, Franz opened the door and saw Martha standing near the bed. Eagerly he approached but Tom kept getting in the way; Martha was laughing and shooing away the dog. Now he saw quite closely her glossy lips, her neck swelling with glee, and he too began to hurry, undoing buttons, pulling a blood-stained bone out of the dog's jaws, and feeling an unbearable sweetness welling up within him; he was about to clasp her hips but suddenly could no longer contain his boiling ecstasy.

Martha sighed and opened her eyes. She thought she had been awakened by a noise in the street: one of their neighbors had a remarkably loud motorcycle. Actually, it was only her husband snoring away with particular abandon. She recalled she had gone to bed without awaiting his return, raised herself, and called to him sharply; then, reaching across the night table, she began roughly tousling his hair, the only trick that worked. His snoring ceased, his lips smacked once or twice. The light on the table flashed on showing the pink of her hand.

"The awakening of the lion," said Dreyer, rubbing his eyes with his fist like a child.

"Where did you go?" Martha asked, glaring at him.

He stared sleepily at her ivory shoulder, at the rose of a bared breast, at the long strand of ebony hair falling on her cheek, and gave a soft chuckle as he slowly leaned back on his pillows.

"I've been showing him Dandy," he muttered cozily. "A night lesson. He can now knot a tie on his paw or his tail. Very entertaining and instructive."

Ah, that was it. Martha felt so relieved, so magnanimous,

that she almost offered . . . but she was also too sleepy. Sleepy and very happy. Without speaking she switched off the light.

"Let's go riding Sunday—what do you say?" a voice murmured tenderly in the dark. But she was already lost in dream. Three lecherous Arabs were haggling over her with a bronze-torsoed handsome slaver. The voice repeated its question in an even more tender, even more questioning tone. A melancholy pause. Then he turned his pillow in quest of a cooler hollow, sighed, and presently was snoring again.

In the morning, as Dreyer was hurriedly enjoying a soft-boiled egg with buttered toast (the most delicious meal known to man) before dashing off to the emporium, Frieda informed him that the repaired car was waiting at the door. Here Dreyer remembered that in the past few days, and particularly after the recent smash, he had repeatedly had a rather amusing thought which he had somehow never brought to its conclusion. But he must act cautiously, in a roundabout manner. A blunt question would lead nowhere. The rascal would leer and deny everything. Would the gardener know? If he did, he would shield him. Dreyer gulped down his coffee and, blinking, poured himself a second cup. Of course, I could be mistaken. . . .

He sipped up the last sweet drop, threw his napkin on the table and hurried out; the napkin slowly crept off the edge of the table and fell limply onto the floor.

Yes, the car had been well repaired. It gleamed with its new coat of black paint, the chrome of its headlight rims, the blazon-like emblem that crested the radiator grill: a silver boy with azure wings. A slightly embarrassed smile bared the chauffeur's ugly gums and teeth as he doffed his blue cap and opened the door. Dreyer glanced at him askance.

"Hello, hello," he said, "so here we are together again." He buttoned all the buttons of his overcoat and continued: "This must have cost a tidy sum—I haven't looked at the bill yet. But that's not the point. I'd be willing to pay even more for the sheer fun of it. A most exhilarating experience, to be sure. Unfortunately, neither my wife nor the police saw the joke."

He tried to think of something else to add, failed, unbuttoned his coat again, and got into the car.

"I gave his physiognomy a thorough examination," he reflected to the accompaniment of the motor's gentle purr. "Still it is impossible to draw any conclusion yet. Of course, his eyes are sort of twinkly, of course, they have those little bags under them. But that may be normal with him. Next time I'll have to take a good sniff."

That morning, as agreed, he visited the emporium and introduced Franz to Mr. Piffke. Piffke was burly, dignified, and smartly dressed. He had blond eyelashes, baby-colored skin, a profile that had prudently stopped halfway between man and teapot, and a second-rate diamond on his plump auricular. He felt for Franz the respect due to the boss's nephew, while Franz gazed with envy and awe at the architectonic perfection of Piffke's trouser creases and the transparent handkerchief peeping out of his breast pocket.

Dreyer did not even mention the lesson of the night before. With his complete approval Piffke assigned Franz not to the tie counter, but to the sporting-goods department. Piffke went to work on Franz with zeal, and his training methods turned out to be very different from Dreyer's, containing as they did a great deal more arithmetic than Franz had expected.

Neither had he expected his feet to ache so much, from constant standing, or his face, from the mechanical expression of affability. As usual in autumn, that part of the emporium was much quieter than the others. Various body-building appliances, ping-pong paddles, striped woollen scarves, soccer boots with black cleats and white laces moved fairly well. The existence of public pools accounted for a continued small demand for bathing suits; but their real season had passed, while the time for skates and skis had not yet come. Thus no rush of customers hampered Franz's training and he had complete leisure to learn his job. His main colleagues were two girls, one red-haired and sharp-nosed, the other a stout energetic blonde inexorably accompanied by a sour smell; and an athletically built young man wearing the same kind of tortoise shell glasses as Franz. He casually informed Franz about the prizes he had won in swimming competitions, and Franz envied him, being himself an excellent swimmer. It was with Schwimmer's help that Franz selected the cloth for two suits and a supply of ties, shirts, and socks. It was he, too, who helped Franz to unravel some minor mysteries of salesmanship far more astutely than Piffke, whose true function was to promenade about the place and grandly arrange meetings between customer and salesman.

During the first few days Franz, dazed and self-conscious, and trying not to shiver (his department was over-ventilated and full of its own athletic drafts), simply stood in a corner trying not to attract attention, avidly following the actions of his colleagues, memorizing their professional movements and intonations, and then abruptly, with unbearable clarity, imagining Martha—the way she had of putting her hand to the back of her chignon, or glancing at her nails and emerald ring. Very soon, however, under the approving solicitous gaze of Mr. Schwimmer, Franz started selling on his own.

He remembered forever his first customer, a stout old man

who asked for a ball. A ball. At once this ball went off bouncing in his imagination, multiplying and scattering, and Franz's head became the playground for all the balls in the store, small, medium, and large—yellow leather ones with stitched sections, fluffy white ones bearing the violet signature of their maker, little black ones hard as stone, extra-light orange-and-blue ones of vacational size, balls of rubber, celluloid, wood, ivory, and they all rolled off in different directions leaving behind a single sphere shining in the middle of his mind when the customer added placidly: "I need a ball for my dog."

"Third shelf on your right, Tooth-Proof," came Schwimmer's prompt whisper, and Franz with a grin of relief and sweat on his brow started to open one wrong box after another but at last found what was needed.

In a month or so he had grown completely accustomed to his work; he no longer got flustered; would boldly bid the inarticulate to repeat their request; and would condescendingly counsel the puny and shy. Fairly well built, fairly broad-shouldered, slim but not skinny, he observed with pleasure his passage in a harem of mirrors and the glances of obviously infatuated shopgirls, and the flash of three silver clips over his heart: Uncle's fountain pen and two pencils, lilac and lead. He might have passed, indeed, for a perfectly respectable, perfectly ordinary salesman, were it not for a blend of details that only a detective of genius might have discerned—a predatory angularity of nostril and cheekbone, a strange weakness about the mouth as if he were always out of breath or had just sneezed, and those eyes, those eyes, poorly disguised by glasses, restless eyes, tragic eyes, ruthless and helpless, of an impure greenish shade with inflamed blood vessels around the iris. But the only detective around was an elderly woman always with the same parcel, who did not bother patrolling Sports but had quite a lot to do in the Neckties department.

Acting upon impeccable Piffke's delicately formulated suggestions, Franz acquired sybarite habits of personal hygiene. He now washed his feet at least twice a week and changed his starched collar and cuffs practically every day. Every evening he brushed his suit and shined his shoes. He used all sorts of nice lotions, smelling of spring flowers and Piffke. He hardly ever skipped his Saturday bath. He put on a clean shirt every Wednesday and Sunday. He made a point of changing his warm underwear at least once in ten days. How shocked his mother would be, he reflected, if she saw his laundry bills!

He accepted with alacrity the tedium of his job, but disliked intensely the necessity of having meals with the rest of the staff. He had hoped that in Berlin he would gradually get over his morbid juvenile squeamishness, but it kept finding mean opportunities to torture him. At table he sat between the plump blonde and the champion swimmer. Whenever she stretched toward the bread basket or the salt, her armpit flooded him with nausea reminding him of a detested spinster teacher at school. The champion on his other side had another infirmity—that of spitting whenever he spoke, and Franz found himself reverting to his schooldays' system of protecting his plate from the spray with forearm and elbow. Only once did he accompany Mr. Schwimmer to the public pool. The water proved to be much too cool and far from clean, and his colleague's roommate, a sunlamp-tanned young Swede, had embarrassing manners.

Basically, though, the emporium, the glossy goods, the brisk or suave dialogue with the customer (who always seemed to be the same actor changing his voice and mask), all this routine was a superficial trickle of repetitive events and sensations which touched him as little as if he was one of those figures of fashion with waxen or wooden faces in suits pressed by the iron of perfection, arrested in a state of colorful putrefaction on their temporary pedestals and platforms, their arms half-bent and half-extended in a parody of pastoral appeal. Young female customers and fleet-footed bob-haired salesgirls from other departments hardly excited him at all. Like the colored commercial stills advertising furniture or furs that succeed each other on the cinema screen for a long time, unaccompanied by music, before a fascinating film starts, all the details of his work were as inevitable as they were trivial. Around six it all stopped abruptly. And then the music would start playing.

Almost nightly—and what monstrous melancholy lurked in that "almost"—he would visit the Dreyers. He dined there only on Sundays, and not every Sunday at that. On weekdays, after a bite at the same cheap restaurant where he had lunched, he took the bus or walked to their villa. A score of evenings had gone by, and everything remained the same: The welcome buzz of the wicket, the pretty lantern illuminating the path through a pattern of ivy, the damp exhalation of the lawn, the gravel's crunch, the tinkle of the doorbell winging off into the house in quest of the maid, the burst of light, Frieda's placid face, and suddenly—life, the tender reverberations of radio music.

She was generally alone; Dreyer, a fantastic but punctual person, would arrive exactly in time for what Franz called supper, and the evening tea, and would always telephone when he thought he might be late. In his presence Franz felt uncomfortable to the point of numbness, and therefore managed to evolve in those days a certain air of grim familiarity in response to Dreyer's natural joviality. But while he was alone with Martha, he had a constant sensation of lan-

guorous pressure somewhere at the top of his spine; his chest
felt tight, his legs weak; his fingers retained for a long time
the cool strength of her handshake. He would compute
within half an inch the exact degree to which she showed
her legs while walking about the room and while sitting with
her legs crossed, and he perceived almost without looking
the tense sheen of her stocking, the swell of her left calf over
the right knee; and the fold of her skirt, sloping, soft, supple,
in which one would have liked to bury one's face. Sometimes, when she got up and walked past him to the radiola,
the light would fall at such an angle as to let the outline of
her thighs show through the light fabric of her skirt, and
once she got a ladder-like run in her stocking and, licking
her finger, quickly dabbed at the silk. Occasionally, the sensation of languid weight became too much for him, and taking advantage of her looking away, he would search her
beauty for some little fault on which he could prop his mind
and sober his fancy, and thus allay the relentless stir of his
senses. Now and then he had the impression that he had
indeed found the saving flaw—a hard line near the mouth, a
pockmark above the eyebrow, a too prominent pout of those
full lips in profile, a dark shadow of down above them, especially noticeable when the powder came off. But one turn of
her head or the slightest change of expression would restore
to her face such adorable charm that he slipped back into
his private abyss even deeper. By means of those rapid
glances he made a complete study of her, followed and fore-
felt her gestures, anticipated the banal but to him unique
movement of her alertly raised hand when one end of a tiny
comb would slacken its grip on her heavy bun. Most of all he
was tormented by the grace and power of her bare white
neck, by that rich delicately grained texture of skin and the
fashionable glimpses of nudity allowed by short flimsy skirts.

[82]

At every new visit he added something to the collection of enchantments which he would gloat over later in his solitary bed, choosing the one his frenzied fancy would work on and spend itself. There was the evening when he saw a minute brown birthmark on her arm. There was the moment when she bent low from her seat to turn back the corner of a rug and he noticed the parting of her breasts and was relieved when the black silk of her bodice became taut again. There was also the night when she was getting ready for a dance, and he was stunned to observe that her armpits were as smooth and white as a statue's.

She questioned him about his childhood, his mother, a dull theme, his native town, an even duller one. Once Tom put his muzzle in Franz's lap and yawned, enveloping him in an unendurable odor—foul herring, carrion. "That is how my childhood smells," muttered Franz as he pushed the dog's head away. She did not hear or did not understand, and asked what he had said. But he did not repeat his confession. He talked about his school, about the dust and the boredom, about his mother's indigestible pies, and about the butcher next door, a dignified gentleman in a white waistcoat who at one time used to come to dinner every day, and eat mutton in a disgustingly professional manner. "Why disgustingly?" Martha interrupted in surprise. "God, what nonsense I'm spouting," he thought, and with mechanical enthusiasm described for the hundredth time the river, the boating, the diving, the beer-drinking under the bridge.

She would switch the radio from song to speech, and he would reverently listen to a Spanish lesson, a lecture on the benefits of athletics, to Mr. Streseman's conciliatory tones, and then—back to some bizarre nasal music. She would tell him in detail the plot of a film, the story of Dreyer's lucky speculations in the days of the inflation, and the gist of an article on the removal of fruit stains. And all the time she would be thinking: "How much longer would he need to get started?" and simultaneously she was amused and even a little touched that he was so unsure of himself and that without her help he would probably never get started at all. Gradually, however, vexation began to predominate. November was being squandered on trifles as money is squandered on trifles when you get stranded in some dull town. With a vague resentment, she recalled that her sister had already had at least four or five lovers in succession, and that Willy Wald's young wife had had two simultaneously. And yet Martha was already past thirty-four. It was high time. In turn, she had been given a husband, a beautiful villa, antique silver, an automobile; the next gift on her list was Franz. Yet it was all not quite so simple; there intruded an alien little breeze, a special ardor, a suspicious softness. . . .

It was no use trying to sleep. Franz opened his window. At the transit from autumn to winter, quirky nights occur when suddenly, out of nowhere, there passes a breath of warm humid air, a belated sigh of summer. He stood in his new zebra pajamas holding on to the window frame, then leaned out, morosely released a long spurt of saliva, and listened, waiting for it to splatter against the sidewalk. However, since he lived on the fifth floor, and not on the second as he had at home, Franz heard nothing. With a slow clatter he shut the window and went back to bed. That night he realized, as one becomes abruptly aware of suffering from a fatal illness, that he had already known Martha for more than two months, and was draining his passion in useless fantasies. And Franz told the pillow, in the half-obscene, half-grandiloquent idiom he affected when talking to himself: "Never mind—better betray my career than wait till my brain cracks. Tomorrow, yes, tomorrow, I'll grab her and tumble her, on the sofa, on the floor, on the table, on broken crockery . . ." Crazy Franz!

Tomorrow came. He went home after work, changed his socks, brushed his teeth, put on his new silk scarf and marched to the bus stop with martial determination. On the way he kept persuading himself that of course she loved him, that only out of pride she concealed her feeling, and that was a pity. If only she leaned toward him as if by chance, and brushed her cheek against his temple over a blurred album, or if she did again, as she had the other night—if she pressed for a moment her back to his before the front-hall mirror and said, turning her perfumed head: "I'm an inch taller than you," or if—but here he pulled himself together and soundlessly told the bus conductor: "That's weakness, and there should be no weakness." Let her be tonight even colder than usual—no matter—now, now, now. . . . As he rang the bell there flashed through his mind a poltroon's hope that perhaps by some chance Dreyer had already come home. Dreyer had not.

As Franz passed through the first two rooms, he pictured how in an instant he would push open that door over there, enter her boudoir, see her in a low-cut black dress with emeralds around her neck, immediately embrace her, hard, make her crunch, make her faint, make her spill her jewels; he pictured it so vividly that for a split second he saw before him his own receding back, saw his hand, saw himself opening the door, and because that sensation was a foray into the future, and it is forbidden to ransack the future, he was swiftly punished. In the first place, as he caught up with himself, he tripped and sent the door flying open. In the second, the room Martha called the boudoir was empty. In the third, when she came in she was wearing a beige dress with a high neck and a long line of buttons. In the fourth place, such a familiar helpless timidity came over him that all he could hope for was to speak more or less articulately.

Martha had decided that tonight he would kiss her for the first time. Characteristically, she chose one of her monthly days lest she succumb too soon, and in the wrong spot, to a yearning that otherwise she could no longer resist. In anticipation of that prudently circumscribed embrace she did not immediately settle down on the sofa near him. As tradition demanded, she turned on the radio, brought a little silver case with Libidettes (Viennese cigarettes), re-arranged the fold of a window curtain, turned on the opal glow of a table lamp, switched off the ceiling light, and (choosing the worst subject imaginable) began telling Franz how the day before Dreyer had started on some mysterious new project—a profitable one, let us hope; she picked up and placed on the back of a chair a pink woollen shawl, and only then gently sat down next to Franz, not quite comfortably folding one leg under her and adjusting the pleats of her skirt.

For no reason at all, he began extolling Uncle, saying how frightfully grateful he was, and how fond he had grown of him. Martha nodded absently. He would alternately puff on his cigarette, or hold it next to his knee, drawing the cardboard tip across the fabric of his trouser leg. The smoke like a flow of spectral milk crept along the clingy nap. Martha extended her hand and with a smile touched his knee as if playing with this phantom larva of smoke. He felt the tender pressure of her fingers. He was hungry, sweaty, and completely impotent.

" . . . And my mother in every letter, you know, sends him her respectful love, her regards, her thanks."

The smoke dissolved. Franz kept sniffing as he did when he was especially nervous. Martha got up and turned off the radio. He lit another cigarette. She had now thrown the pink shawl over her shoulders and, like a woman in some old-fashioned romance, gazed at him fixedly from the far corner of the settee. With a wooden laugh, he recounted an anecdote from yesterday's paper. Then, nudging the door with his paw, a very sad, very sleek, very hopeless Tom appeared, and Franz for the first time actually talked to the astonished animal. And at last, thank God, beloved Dreyer arrived.

Franz came home around eleven, and as he was proceeding along the passage on tiptoe to the foul little water closet he heard a chuckle coming from the landlord's door. The door was ajar. He peeped into the room as he passed. Old Enricht, clad only in his nightshirt, was standing on all fours with his wrinkled and hoary rear toward a brilliant cheval glass. Bending low his congested face, fringed with white hair, like the head of the professor in the "Hindu Prince" farce, he was peering back through the archway of his bare thighs at the reflection of his bleak buttocks.

5

There was indeed an air of mystery about Dreyer's new project. It all began one Wednesday in mid-November when he received a visit from a nondescript stranger with a cosmopolitan name and no determinable origin. He might have been Czech, Jewish, Bavarian, Irish—it was entirely a matter of personal evaluation.

Dreyer was sitting in his office (a huge quiet place with huge unquiet windows, with a huge desk, and huge leather armchairs) when, having traversed an olive-green corridor past glass expanses full of the hurricane-like clatter of typewriters, this nondescript gentleman was ushered in. He was hatless but wore a topcoat and warm gloves.

The card that had preceded him by a couple of minutes bore the title of "Inventor" under his name. Now Dreyer was fond, perhaps over-fond, of inventors. With a mesmeric gesture, he deposited his guest in the leathern luxury of an over-stuffed chair (with an ashtray affixed to its giant paw) and, toying with a red-and-blue pencil, sat down half-facing him. The man's thick eyebrows wiggled like furry black caterpillars, and the freshly shaven parts of his melancholy face had a dark turquoise cast.

The inventor began from afar, and this Dreyer approved. All business ought to be handled with that artful caution. Lowering his voice, the inventor passed with laudable smoothness from the preface to the substance. Dreyer laid down his pencil. Suavely and in detail the Magyar—or Frenchman, or Pole—stated his business.

"You say, then, that it has nothing to do with wax?" asked Dreyer. The inventor raised his finger. "Absolutely nothing, though I call it 'voskin,' a trade name that will be in all dictionaries tomorrow. Its main component is a resilient, colorless product resembling flesh. I particularly stress its elasticity, its pliability, its rippliability, so to speak."

"Speak by all means," said Dreyer. "And what about that 'electric impellent'—I don't quite understand; what do you mean, for example, by 'contractive transmission'?"

The inventor smiled a wise smile. "Ah, that's the whole point. Obviously, it would be much simpler if I showed you the blueprints; but it is also obvious that I'm not yet inclined to do so. I have explained how you can apply my invention. Now it's up to you to give me the funds for the construction of the first sample."

"How much would you need?" asked Dreyer with curiosity.

The inventor replied in detail.

"Don't you think," said Dreyer with a mischievous glint in his eye, "that perhaps your imagination is worth much more? I highly respect and value the imagination in others. If for example a man came to me and said: 'My dear *Herr Direktor*, I would like to dream a little. How much will you pay me for dreaming?' then, maybe, I would begin negotiations with him. Whereas you, my dear inventor, you offer at once something practical, factory production and so forth. Who cares about realization? I am duty-bound to believe in

[89]

a dream but to believe in the embodiment of that dream—
Puh!" (one of Dreyer's lipbursts).

At first the inventor did not understand; then he understood and was offended.

"In other words, you simply refuse?" he asked gloomily.

Dreyer sighed. The inventor clucked his tongue, and
leaned back in his chair clasping and unclasping his hands.

"This is my life's work," he said at last, staring into space.
"Like Hercules, I have been struggling with the tentacles of
a dream for ten years, mastering this softness, this flexibility,
this plexibility, this stylized animation, if I may use the expression."

"*Of course* you may," said Dreyer. "I'd even say that's
better than the—what was it—'ripplexibility'? Tell me," he
began, picking up the pencil again—a good sign (though his
interlocutor could not know it), "have you approached anyone else with that offer?"

"Well," said the inventor with perfectly mimicked sin-
cerity, "I confess this is the first time. In fact, I have just
arrived in Germany. This *is* Germany, isn't it?" he added,
looking around.

"So I'm told," said Dreyer.

There was a fruit-bearing pause.

"Your dream is enchanting," said Dreyer pensively, "enchanting."

The other grimaced and flared up: "Stop harping on
dreams, sir. They have come true, they have become flesh, in
more senses than one, even though I may be a pauper, and
cannot build my Eden and eidolons. Have you ever read
Epicritus?"

Dreyer shook his head.

"Nor have I. But do give me a chance to prove that I am
no quack. They told me you were interested in such innova-

tions. Just think what a delight this would be, what an adornment, what an astounding, and permit me to say even artistic, achievement."

"What guarantee do you offer me?" asked Dreyer, relishing the entertainment.

"The guarantee of the human spirit," the inventor said trenchantly.

Dreyer laughed. "That's more like it. You revert to my original viewpoint."

He thought for a moment, then added: "I think I want to roll your offer around in my head. Who knows, maybe I'll see your invention in my next dream. My imagination must become steeped in it. At the moment I can say neither yes nor no. Now run along home. Where are you staying?"

"Hotel Montevideo," said the inventor. "An idiotically misleading name."

"But also a familiar one, though I can't remember why. Video, video. . . ."

"I see you have my friend's Pugowitz Tapwater Filter," said the inventor, pointing at the faucet in the corridor with the air of Rembrandt indicating a Claude Lorraine.

"Video, video," repeated Dreyer. "No, I don't know. Well, ponder our talk. Decide if you really want to kill a delightful fancy by selling it to the factory, and in a week or ten days I'll ring you up. And—pardon me for alluding to this—I hope you'll be a bit more communicative, a bit more trusting."

When his visitor had left, Dreyer sat motionless, his hands thrust deep into his trouser pockets. "No, he is not a charlatan," he reflected. "Or at least he is not aware of being one. Why not have a little fun? If it is all he says, the results really may be curious." The telephone emitted a discreet buzz, and for a time he forgot about the inventor.

That evening, however, he hinted to Martha that he was about to embark on a completely new project, and when she asked if it were profitable, he narrowed his eyes and nodded: "Oh, very, very profitable, my love." Next morning, as he was snorting under the shower, he decided not to receive the inventor again. At lunchtime, in a restaurant, he remembered him with pleasure and decided that the invention was something unique and irresistible. Upon coming home to supper he remarked to Martha casually that the project had fallen through. She was wearing her beige dress and was wrapped in a pink shawl, though it was quite warm in the house. Franz, whom he considered an amusing simpleton, was as usual jumpy and gloomy. He soon went home, saying he had smoked too much and had a headache. As soon as he had gone, Martha went up to the bedroom. In the boudoir on the tripod table by the sofa a silver box remained open. Dreyer took a Libidette from it and burst out laughing. "Contractive transmission! Animated flexibility! No, he can't be cheating. I think his idea is awfully attractive."

When he in turn went up to bed, Martha seemed to be asleep. After several centuries had elapsed, the bed table lamp went out. Presently she opened her eyes and listened. He was snoring. She lay on her back, gazing into the dark. Everything irritated her—that snoring, that gleam in the dark, probably in the looking glass, and incidentally, her own self.

"That was the wrong approach," she thought. "Tomorrow night I'll take drastic measures. Tomorrow night."

Franz, however, did not appear either the next evening or on Saturday. On Friday he had gone to a movie, and on Saturday, to a café with his colleague Schwimmer. At the cinema, an actress with a little black heart for lips and with eyelashes like the spokes of an umbrella was impersonating a rich heiress impersonating a poor office girl. The café turned out to be dark and dull. Schwimmer kept talking about the goings-on among boys in summer camps, and a rouged whore with a repulsive gold tooth was looking at them and swinging her leg, and half-smiling at Franz every time she shook off the ash of her cigarette.

It would have been so simple, thought Franz, to grasp her when she touched my knee. Agony. . . . Should I perhaps wait a while and not see her for a few days? But then life is not worth living. The next time I swear, yes, I swear. I swear by my mother and sister.

On Sunday his landlord brought him his coffee as usual at nine-thirty. Franz did not at once dress and shave as he did on weekdays, but merely pulled on his old dressing gown over his pajamas, and sat down at the table to write his weekly letter: "Dear Mama," he wrote in his crawling hand, "how are you? How is Emmy? Probably . . . —"

He paused, crossed out the last word and lapsed into thought, picking his nose, looking at the rainy day in the window. Probably they were on their way to church now. In the afternoon there would be coffee with whipped cream. He imagined his mother's fat florid face and dyed hair. What did she care about him? She had always loved Emmy more. She had still boxed his ears when he was seventeen, eighteen, even nineteen—last year, in fact. Once at Easter, when he was quite small but already bespectacled, she had ordered him to eat a little chocolate bunny that had been well licked by his sister. For having licked the candy meant for him Emmy received a light slap on the behind, but to him, for having refused to touch the slimy brown horror, she delivered such a backhand whack in the face that he flew off his chair, hit his head against the sideboard and lost consciousness. His love for his mother was never very deep but even so it was his first unhappy love, or rather he regarded her as a rough draft of a first love, for although he had craved for her affection because his schoolbooks of stories (*My Soldier Boy, Hanna Comes Home*) told him, as they had from immemorial time, that mothers always doted upon their sons and daughters, he actually could not stand her physical appearance, mannerisms, and emanations, the depressing, depressingly familiar odor of her skin and clothes, the bedbug-brown fat birthmark on her neck, the trick she had of scratching with a knitting needle the unappetizing parting of her chestnut hair, her enormous dropsical ankles, and all the kitchen faces she made by which he could unerringly determine what she was preparing—beer soup or bull hodes, or that dreadful local dainty *Budenzucker*.

Perhaps—in retrospection, at least—he had suffered less from her indifference, meanness, fits of temper, than from the embarrassment and detestation when she pinched his cheek in feigned fondness before a guest, usually the next-door butcher, or in the latter's presence forced him in folly and fun to kiss his sister's schoolmate Christina whom he adored from a distance, and to whom he would have apologized for those dreadful moments had she paid the least attention to him. Perhaps, in spite of everything, his mother missed him now? She never wrote anything about her feelings in her infrequent letters.

Still it was nice to feel sorry for oneself, it brought hot tears to one's eyes. And Emmy—she was a good girl. She would marry the butcher's assistant. Best butcher in town. Damn this rain. Dear Mama. What else? Maybe a description of the room?

He replaced his right slipper, which had aged more quickly than the left one and kept falling off his foot when he dangled it, and looked around.

"As I already wrote you, I have an excellent room, but I never described it to you properly. It has a mirror and a washstand. Above the bed there is the beautiful picture of a lady in an Oriental setting. The wallpaper has brownish flowers. In front of me, against the wall, there is a chest-of-drawers."

At that moment there came a light knock, Franz turned his head, and the door opened a crack. Old Enricht thrust his head in, winked, disappeared, and said to somebody on the other side of the door: "Yes, he is at home. Go right in."

She was wearing her beautiful moleskin coat thrown open over a veily, vapory dress; the rain that had caught her between taxi and entrance had had time to dot with dark stains her pearl-gray helmet-like hat; she stood pressing closely together her legs in apricot silk, as if on a parade. Still standing thus, she reached behind her and closed the door. She took off her gloves. Intently, unsmilingly, she stared at Franz as if she had not expected to see him. He covered his bare Adam's apple with his hand and uttered a long sentence but noticed with surprise that seemingly no words had been produced, as if he had tapped them out on a typewriter in which he had forgotten to insert a ribbon.

"Excuse me for bursting in like this," said Martha, "but I was afraid you might be ill."

Palpitating and blinking, his lower lip drooping, Franz began helping her to get rid of her coat. The silk lining was crimson, as crimson as lips and flayed animals, and smelled of heaven. He placed her coat and hat on the bed, and one last staunch little observer in the storm of his consciousness, after the rest of his thoughts had scattered, noted that this was like a train passenger marking the seat he is about to occupy.

In the dining room they sat facing each other across the table. Dreyer was finishing what remained of the cold chicken. Martha, her face pale and glossy, with drops of sweat over her lip where the tiny black hairs showed, stared with her fingers pressed to her temples at the white, white, intolerably white tablecloth.

7

When the inevitable explosion (somehow sensed as inevitable just before it occurred) was on the point of interrupting an absorbing although incoherent conversation with an unshaven Magyar or Basque about treating surgically, with buckets of blood, a seal's tail to enable the seal to walk upright, Dreyer abruptly returned to the mortality of a winter morning, and with desperate haste, as if he were dealing with an infernal machine, stopped the alarm clock that was about to ring.

Martha's bed was already empty. A bad tingle in his left arm connected like an electric buzzer the previous day with the present one. Along the corridor, sobbing loudly, shuffled soft-hearted Frieda. With a sigh he examined the huge violet bruise on his thick shoulder.

While lying in the tub, he heard Martha perform in the next room the panting, crunching, flopping exercises that were in fashion that year. He had a quick breakfast, lit a cigar, smiled with pain as he put on his overcoat, and went out.

The gardener (who was also the watchman) was standing by the fence, and Dreyer thought it might be well, even at this late date, to solve by means of a direct question the mystery that had preoccupied him for so long.

"A calamity, a real calamity," observed the gardener gravely. "And to think that back in his village he has left a comparatively young father and four little sisters. A skid on the ice, and *kaputt*. He had hoped so much to drive a big truck some day."

"Yes," nodded Dreyer. "Cracked his skull, his rib cage—"

"A good merry chap," said the gardener with feeling. "And now he is dead."

"Listen," began Dreyer, "you did not happen to notice— You see, I have a strong suspicion—"

He faltered. A trifle—the tense of a verb—stopped him. Instead of asking "does he drink?" it would have to be "did he drink?" This shift of tense caused a wobble in logic.

" . . . as I was saying, have you noticed—there is something wrong with the latch of the big parlor window. I mean, the catch does not work properly; anybody could get in from the outside."

"*Finis*," he mused, as he sat in a taxi with his hand in the strap. "The end of a life, the end of a joke. I shall sell Icarus without repairing it. She does not want another car, and I think she is right. It's best to wait awhile till Fate forgets."

The reason Martha did not want a car was less metaphysical. It might seem a bit strange and suspicious not to use one's own car to go two or three times a week in the late afternoon to lessons in rhythmic inclinations and gesticulations ("Flora, accept these lilies" or "Let us unfold our veils in the wind"), and the reason she could not use it was that she would have to bribe her chauffeur to be silent about her real destination. Therefore she had to resort to other means of transportation, of the most varied kind, including even the subway, which brought one very conveniently from any part of the city (and a roundabout route was essential though it took only fifteen minutes to walk the distance) to a certain street corner where a rather fantastic house was being slowly built. She casually mentioned to Dreyer that she loved taking a bus or a tram whenever she had a chance because it was a shame not to take advantage of the cheap, exhilaratingly cheap, methods of transportation put at one's disposal by a generous city. He said he was a generous citizen who preferred a taxi or a private car. By taking these precautions, Martha believed that nobody would ever guess that she transposed or curtailed or missed altogether those delightful contortions and scattering of invisible flowers in the delightful company of other barefooted ladies in more or less comical tunics.

On the day that businessman Dreyer, owner of the Dandy department store, and his chauffeur briefly appeared in the city news section of her newspaper, Martha arrived a little earlier than usual. Franz was not yet back from work. She sat down on the couch, took off her hat, slowly removed her gloves. That day her face was particularly pale. She wore her high-neck beige dress with little buttons in front. When Franz's familiar footsteps sounded in the corridor and he entered (with that abrupt unceremoniousness with which we enter our own room, assuming that it is empty), she did not smile. Franz emitted an exclamation of pleased surprise and without taking off his hat began to shower Martha's neck and ear with rapid kisses.

"You know about it already?" she asked, and her eyes had the strange expression he had hoped never to see again.

"You bet," he answered and, getting up from the couch, shed his raincoat and striped scarf. "Everybody was discussing it at the store. They asked me all kinds of questions. I was really scared when he came in looking so grim yesterday. What a dreadful thing."

"What's dreadful, Franz?"

He was already coatless and collarless, and was noisily washing his hands.

"Well, all that jagged glass hitting you in the face, that crunch of metal and bones, and blood, and blackness. I don't know why but I picture such things so clearly. Makes me want to vomit."

"That is just nerves, Franz, nerves. Come here."

He sat down close to her and, trying not to notice that she was absorbed in remote dreary thoughts of her own, softly asked:

"No pompons today?"

She did not hear the sweet euphemism, or did not seem to hear it.

"Franz," she said, stroking and restraining his hand, "do you realize what a miracle it was? I had a presentiment yesterday which did not work."

"There we go again," he thought, "how long will she bore me with her concern for him?"

He turned away and attempted to whistle, but no sound came out and he remained brooding with puckered lips.

"What's the matter with you, Franz? Stop acting like a fool. I'm closed for repairs today" (another sweet euphemism).

She drew him to her by the neck; he would not yield but her diamond-like gaze slashed him, and he went all limp and whimpery, the way a child's balloon collapses with a pitiful squeak. Tears of resentment fogged his glasses. He pressed his head to her shoulder: "I can't go on like this," he whined. "Already last night I wondered if your feeling for me was really serious. Worrying about that old uncle of mine! It means you care for him! Oh, it's so painful—"

Martha blinked, then understood his mistake. "So that's what it is," she drawled with a laugh. "Oh, you poor dear."

She took his head in her hands, looked intently and sternly into his eyes, and then slowly, with her mouth half open, as if she were about to give him a gentle bite, drew close to his face, and took possession of his lips.

"Shame on you," she said, releasing him slowly, "shame on you," she repeated with a nod. "I never thought you were that silly. No, just a minute—I want you to understand how silly you are. No, wait. You can't touch me but I can certainly touch you, and nibble you, and even swallow you whole if I want."

"Listen," she said a little while later, after that stunt, quite new to Franz, had been brought to a satisfactory close. "Listen, Franz, how wonderful it would be if I didn't have to go today. Today, or tomorrow, or ever. Of course, we could not live in a tiny room like this."

"We would rent a larger, brighter room," said Franz with assurance.

"Yes. Let's dream a little. Larger and much brighter. Maybe even two rooms, what do you think? Or perhaps three? And of course a kitchen."

"And lots of beautiful knives," said Franz, "meat cleavers, and cheese cutters, and a roast pork slicer, but you would not do any cooking. You have such precious nails."

"Yes, naturally, we'd have a cook. What did we decide—three rooms?"

"No, four," said Franz after a moment's thought. "Bedroom, drawing room, sitting room, dining room."

"Four. Fine. A regular four-room apartment. With kitchen. With bath. And we'll have the bedroom all done in white, won't we? And the other rooms blue. And there'll be a reception room with lots and lots of flowers. And an extra room upstairs, just in case, for guests, say. . . . For a wee little guest, maybe."

"What do you mean—'upstairs'?"

"Why, of course—it will be a villa."

"Ah, I see," nodded Franz.

"Let's continue, darling. A detached villa, then. With a pretty entrance hall. We enter. Rugs, pictures, silverware, embroidered sheets. Right? And a garden, fruit trees. Magnolias. Is that so, Franz?"

He sighed. "All this will come only in ten years, or more. It will be a long time before I earn sufficiently for you to divorce him."

Martha fell silent as if she were not in the room. Franz turned to her with a smile, ready to play on, but the smile faded: she was looking at him with narrowed eyes, biting her lip.

"Ten years," she said bitterly. "You little fool! You really want to wait ten years?"

"That's how it looks to me," Franz replied. "I don't know. Maybe, if I'm very lucky . . . but, for instance, take Mr. Piffke; he's been with the store right from the start, and that's you know how many years. But he lives very modestly. He doesn't make more than four hundred fifty a month. His wife works too. They have a tiny apartment full of boxes and things."

"Thank God you understand," said Martha. "You see, sweetheart, one cannot deposit dreams at the bank. They aren't dependable securities, and the dividends they bring are nothing."

"Then what shall we do?" said frightened Franz. "You know I'm ready to marry you immediately. I can't exist without you. Without you I'm like an empty sleeve. But I can't even afford one of those nice new floormats we sell at the store, let alone carpets. And then, of course, I'd have to look for another job—and I don't know anything (wrinkling his face), I have no experience in anything. That means learning all over again. We'd have to live in a damp, shabby little room, saving on food and clothes."

"Yes, there would be no longer any uncle to help," said Martha dryly. "No uncle at all."

"The whole idea is unthinkable," said Franz.

"Absolutely unthinkable," said Martha.

"Why are you angry with me?" he asked after a moment's silence. "As if I were responsible or something. It's really not my fault. Well, let's dream on, if you want. Only don't get angry. I have seventeen suits, like Uncle— Want me to describe them for you?"

"In ten years," she said with a laugh, "in ten years, my dear, men's fashions will have changed substantially."

"There—you are angry again."

"Yes, I'm angry; not with you, though, but with Fate. You see, Franz—no, you wouldn't understand."

"I'll understand," said Franz.

"All right then. You see, people generally make all kinds of plans, very good plans, but completely fail to consider one possibility: death. As if no one could ever die. Oh, don't look at me as if I were saying something indecent."

She now had exactly the same odd expression as last night when she tried to impersonate a policeman.

"It's time for me to go," said Martha with a frown. She got up and looked at herself in the mirror.

"Christmas trees are already sold in the streets," she said, raising her elbows as she put on her hat. "I want to buy a tree, a huge very expensive fir tree, and lots of presents to go under it. Please, give me four hundred and twenty marks. I'm out of pocket."

"And you're also very nasty," sighed Franz.

He accompanied her down the dark stairs. He walked her to the square. The builders had started on the facade of the new cinema. The sidewalk was very slippery, the glare ice glistened under the street lamps.

"You know something, treasure?" she said when bidding him good-by at the corner. "I might have been in deep mourning today. And very becoming it would have been. It's just by chance that I'm not in mourning. Ponder that, my little nephew."

Exactly what she wanted happened then: Franz looked at her, opened his mouth, and suddenly burst out laughing. She rocked with laughter, too. A gentleman with a fox terrier, who was waiting near by for the dog to make up its mind in regard to a lamppost, glanced at the merry couple with approval and envy. "In mourning," said Franz, choking with laughter. She nodded, laughing. "In mourning," said Franz, stifling a rich guffaw in the palm of his hand. The man with the fox terrier shook his head and moved on. "I adore you," uttered Franz in a weak voice, and for quite a while gazed after her with moist eyes.

However, as soon as she turned away to go home Martha's face again grew stern. Franz meanwhile wiped his glasses with his handkerchief and ambled off, continuing to chuckle to himself. "Yes, it really was a matter of chance. If only the owner of the car had sat beside the chauffeur. Just supposing he'd gone and sat there. There she would be today—a widow. A rich widow, an adorable mistress, a wonderful wife. How drolly she put it: yours is honey; his, poison. And then again, who needs an elaborate crack-up. After all, car accidents are not necessarily fatal; much too often one gets away with bruises, a fracture, lacerations, one mustn't make too complicated demands on chance: exactly that way, please, make the brains squirt out. There are other possibilities: illnesses, for example. Perhaps he has a bad heart and does not know it. And look at all the influenza people who croak. Then we'd really start living. The store would go on doing business. The money would roll in. But then more likely he'll outlive his wife and make it all the way to the twenty-first century. Why, there was something in the papers about a Turk who was a hundred and fifty years old, and still produced children, the filthy old brute."

Thus he mused, vaguely and crudely, unaware that his thoughts were spinning along from the push given them by Martha. The thought of marriage had also come from her. Oh, but it was a good thought. If he derived such pleasure from Martha's satisfying him twice in one hour three or four times a week, what varied ecstasies would she grant him if she were available twenty-four hours a day! He employed this method of calculating happiness quite guilelessly, the way a greedy child imagines a country with chocolate-cream mud and ice-cream snow.

In those days—which as a very old and very sick man, guilty of worse sins than avunculicide, he remembered with a grin of contempt—young Franz was oblivious to the corrosive probity of his pleasant daydreams about Dreyer's dropping dead. He had plunged into a region of delirium, blithely and light-heartedly. His subsequent meetings with Martha appeared to be as natural and tender as all the previous ones but, just as that modest little room, with its unpretentious old furniture and its naively dark corridor, had for master a person, or persons, incurably though not obviously insane, there now lurked in those meetings something strange—a little eerie and shameful at first, but already enthralling, already all-powerful. Whatever Martha said, however charmingly she smiled, Franz sensed an irresistible insinuation in her every word and glance. They were like heirs sitting in a dim-lit parlor while in the bedroom doomed Plutus pleads with the doctor and curses the priest; they might talk about trifles, about the approach of Christmas, about the intense activity of skis and wool at the emporium; one might talk about anything although perhaps a little more soberly than before—for one's hearing is strained, one's eyes have a changeable gleam; a secret impatience allows one no peace as one waits and waits for the grim physician to come out on tiptoe, with an eloquent sigh, and lo— through the crack of the door one glimpses the long back of the cleric, representative of a boundlessly charitable Church, in the act of bending over the white, white bed.

Theirs was a pointless vigil. Martha knew perfectly well that he never seemed to have even so much as a toothache or a cold. Therefore it was particularly irritating to her when just before the holidays she herself contracted a chill; the poor girl developed a dry cough, a tease and a wheeze in the bronchia, night sweats, and spent the day in a kind of dull trance, dazed by the so-called *Grippe*, heavy-headed and with ears abuzz. When Christmas came she felt no better. That evening, nevertheless, she put on a sheer flame-colored dress, very low cut at the back; and deafened by aspirin, trying to dispell her illness by will power, supervised the preparation of the punch, the laying of the table, the ruddy smoky activity of the cook.

In the parlor, its silvery crown touching the ceiling, all decked out in flimsy tinselry, all studded with still unlit red and blue bulbs, a fresh luxuriant fir tree stood, indifferent to its buffoonish array. In an uncozy nook between the parlor and the entry, a bright and rather bare place, termed for some reason a reception room, where among the wicker furniture grew and bloomed potted plants—cyclamens, seven dwarf cactuses, a peperomia with painted leaves—and where the tangerine glow of an electric fireplace could not beat the draft from a plate-glass window, Dreyer in evening dress sat reading an English book while waiting for his guests. The scene was laid on the Island of Capri. He moved his lips as he read and peeked pretty often into a fat dictionary which kept shuttling between his lap and a glass-topped table. Not knowing what to do with herself during this prolonged lull before the first ring, Martha sat down at a little distance from him on a settee and lifted her foot off the floor, examining from every angle her pointed shoe. The stillness was intolerable. Dreyer accidentally dropped the dictionary and, making his generously starched shirt crackle, retrieved it without taking his eyes off his book. What could she do with that oppression, that tightness in the chest? Coughing alone could not relieve it; there was only one thing that could make the whole world well: the sudden and total disappearance of that self-satisfied bulky man with the leonine brows and freckled hands. The acuteness of her hatred reached such a pitch of perception that for a moment she had the illusion that his chair was empty. But his cuff link described a flashing arc as he shut the dictionary, and he said, smiling at her consolingly: "Goodness, what a cold you have. I can hear a veritable orchestra of wheezes tuning up in you."

"Spare me your metaphors and put your book away," said Martha. "The guests will be here any moment. And that dictionary. There's nothing more untidy than a dictionary on a chair."

"*All right, my treasury,*" he answered in English, and

walked away with his books, mentally lamenting his unsure pronunciation and meager though exact vocabulary.

The chair by the glowing grate now stood empty, but that did not help. With her whole being she experienced his presence, there, behind the door, in the next room, and the next, and the next; the house was suffocating from him; the clocks ticked with an effort and the cold folded napkins stood stifling on the festive table with a strangled rose in each individual vase—but how to cough him up, how to breathe freely again? It now seemed to her that it had always been thus, that she had hated him hopelessly since the first days and nights of their marriage when he kept pawing and licking her like an animal, in a locked hotel room in white Salsborg. He now stood in her path, in her plain, straight path, like a solid obstacle, that ought somehow to be removed to let her resume her plain straight existence. How dared he enforce upon her the complications of adultery? How dared he stand in the queue before her? Our cruellest enemy is less hateful than the burley stranger whose placid back keeps us from squeezing through to a ticket window or to the counter of a sausage shop. She walked to and fro, she drummed on a window. She tore off a diseased cyclamen leaf, she felt she would suffocate any moment. At that instant the doorbell sounded. Martha checked her hairdo and walked quickly—not to the front door but back to the door of the drawing room in order to make an elegant entrance from afar to meet her guests.

During the next half hour the bell rang again and again. First to arrive were the inevitable Walds in their Debler limousine; then came Franz shivering from the cold; then, almost simultaneously, the count with a bouquet of mediocre pinks and a paper manufacturer with his wife; then—

two loud, half-naked, ill-groomed girls whose late father had been their host's partner in happier days; then—the snub-nosed, gaunt, and taciturn director of the Fatum Insurance Company; and a rosy-cheeked civil engineer in triplicate—that is, with a sister and a son comically resembling him. All this company gradually warmed up and coalesced until it formed a single many-limbed but otherwise not over-complex creature that made mirthful noise, and drank, and whirled. Only Martha and Franz were unable to identify themselves, as they should have by all the laws of a hearty holiday, with this animated, flushed, palpitating mass. She was pleased to note how unresponsive Franz was to the practically naked charms of those two practically identical vulgar young things with revoltingly thin arms, and snaky backs, and insufficiently spanked little popos. The injustice of life—in ten years' time they would be still a little younger than I am now, all three of them as a matter of fact.

Every now and then her eyes and those of Franz would meet, but even without looking he and she always clearly sensed the changing correlation of their respective where-abouts: while he walked diagonally across the parlor with a glass of punch for Ida or Isolda—no, for old Mrs. Wald—Martha was putting a rustling paper hat on bald Willy at the other end of the room; as Franz sat down and started listen-ing to what the engineer's sister, pink-cheeked and plain, had to say, Martha combined the oblique and the straight line by going from Willy to the door, and then to the din-ing-room table laden with hors-d'oeuvres. Franz lit a ciga-rette, Martha put a mandarin on a plate. Thus a chess player playing blind feels his trapped bishop and his opponent's versatile queen move in relentless relation to each other. There was a vaguely regular rhythm established in those coordinations. And not for an instant was it interrupted. She and especially Franz felt the existence of this invisible geometric figure; they were two points moving through it, and the interrelation between those two points could be plotted at any given moment; and though they seemed to move independently they were nonetheless securely bound by the invisible, inexorable lines of that figure.

The parquet was already littered with motley paper trash; already someone had broken a glass and stood speechless with sticky fingers outspread. Willy Wald, already high, wearing a golden hat and garlanded with paper ribbons, his innocent blue eyes opened wide, was recounting to the gruff old count his recent trip to Russia, ardently extolling the Kremlin, the caviar, the commissars. Presently Dreyer, coatless, flushed, still holding a chef's knife and wearing a chef's cap, took Willy aside and began whispering something to him, while the rosy engineer went on telling the other guests about three masked individuals who, one Christmas night, had broken in and robbed the whole company. The phonograph broke into song in the adjoining boudoir. Dreyer started to dance with one of the pretty sisters, and then caught up the other, and the girls giggled and curved their supple bare backs as he tried to dance with both together. Franz stood by the window drapery, regretting that he still had not had time to learn to dance. He saw Martha's white hand on somebody's black shoulder, then her profile, then the birthmark under her left shoulder blade and somebody's thumb upon it, then the madonna profile again, and again the raisin in the cream; and her silk-sheening legs which the hem of her short skirt revealed up to the knee moved hither and thither, and seemed (if one looked at them only) to belong to a woman who did not know what to do with herself from restlessness and anticipation: she steps, now slowly, now quickly, this way and that, turns abruptly, steps

again in her excruciating impatience. Martha danced automatically, feeling not so much the rhythm of the music as
the syncopic changes between her and Franz, who was
standing by the drapery with folded arms and moving eyes.
She noticed Dreyer reach through the drapery; he must have
opened the window a little, for it grew cooler in the room.
As she danced, she kept checking Franz's position: he was
there, the dear sentinel; she searched for her husband with
her eyes; he had left the room and she told herself that the
sudden coolness and well-being were due precisely to his
absence. On gliding closer to Franz she bathed him in such a
familiar meaningful look that he lost countenance and
smiled at the engineer whose face was presented to him by
the whim of a whirl. Again and again the phonograph was
wound, and among many pairs of ordinary legs flashed those
strong, graceful, ravishing legs, and Franz, dizzy from the
wine and the gyrations of the dancers, became aware of a
certain terpsichorean tumult in his poor head as if all his
thoughts were learning to foxtrot.

Then something happened. In mid-dance Isolda cried:
"Oh, look! The drape!"

Everyone looked, and, indeed, the window curtain stirred
strangely, altered its folds, and swelled slowly. Simultaneously the lights went out. In the darkness an oval light began
to move about the room, the drapery parted, and in the
unsteady glimmer, a masked man suddenly appeared,
dressed in an old military coat and carrying a menacing
flashlight in his fist. Ida gave a piercing scream. The engineer's voice calmly pronounced in the dark: "I suspect that's
our genial host." Then, after a curious pause, filled by the
phonograph which had gone on dutifully playing in the
dark, there sounded Martha's tragic voice. She gave such a
howl of warning that the two girls and the old count surged

back toward the door (blocked by merry Willy). The masked figure emitted a hoarse sound and, training the light on Martha, moved forward. It is possible that the girls were genuinely frightened. It is also possible that one or two of the men were beginning to doubt its being a prank. Martha, who went on crying for help, noticed with cold exultation that the engineer standing beside her had reached back under his dinner jacket and had produced something from his hip pocket. She realized what her screams meant, what prompted them, and what they should cause to happen; and, secure in her performance, she screamed still louder, urging, hallooing.

Franz could not bear it any longer. He stood nearest of all to the intruder, had recognized him at once by his tailor-made tuxedo trousers, and now his nimble fingers ripped the mask off the intruder's face. Meanwhile Mr. Fatum had finally overcome panting Willy and switched on the lights. In the center of the room, dressed in a combination of apache scarf and soldier's coat, stood Dreyer roaring with laughter, now swaying, now squatting, all red and tousled, and pointing his finger at Martha. Quickly deciding how she should now resolve her feigned terror, she turned her back upon her husband, re-arranged the strap on one bare shoulder, and calmly went off to the faltering phonograph. He rushed after her and, still laughing, hugged and kissed her. "Oh, I knew it was you all along," she said—which, of course, was quite true.

Franz had been trying for some time to fight off the welling of nausea but now he was going to be sick, and he hurriedly left the room. Behind him the hubbub continued; they were all laughing and shouting, probably crowding around Dreyer, squeezing him, squeezing him, squeezing both him and Martha, who wriggled. With his handkerchief pressed to his lips, Franz made for the front hall, and wrenched open the door of the toilet. Old Mrs. Wald came flying out like a bomb and disappeared behind the bend of the wall. "My God, my God," he muttered, doubled over. He emitted horrible sounds, recognizing in the intermittent torrent a medley of food and drink the way a sinner in hell retastes the hash of his life. Breathing heavily, squeamishly wiping his mouth with a bit of toilet paper, he waited for a moment, and pulled the chain. On his way back he paused in the entrance hall and listened. Through an open door a mirror reflected the ominously blazing Christmas tree. The phonograph was singing again. Suddenly he saw Martha.

She went up to him quickly, looking over her shoulder like a conspirator in a play. They were alone in the brightly lit hall, and from beyond the door came noise, laughter, the squeals of a helpless pig, the quawks of a tortured turkey.

"No luck," said Martha. "I'm sorry, dear."

Her piercing eyes were at once in front of him and all around him. Then she started to cough, clutched at her side and dropped in a chair.

He asked: "What do you mean—no luck?"

"It cannot go on like this," muttered Martha between fits of coughing. "It simply cannot. Why, look at yourself— you're as pale as death."

The noise in the house was swelling and drawing nearer; it seemed as though that enormous tree were bellowing with all its lights.

" . . . as death," said Martha.

Franz felt another onset of nausea; the voices surged forward; sweaty Dreyer rushed past, escaping from Wald and the engineer, and after them came the others guffawing and gibbering, and Tom, locked up in the garage, was barking his head off. And the noise of the hunt seemed to pursue

Franz as he vomited in the deserted street and staggered home. At the corner of the square the scaffolding that cocooned the future Kino-Palazzo was adorned on the very top with a bright Christmas tree. The latter could be also seen, but only as a tiny colored blur in the starry sky from the Dreyers' bedroom window.

"Either of the two would make a marvellous little wife for good old Franz," said Dreyer as he undressed.

"That's what you think," said Martha, glaring into her dressing-table mirror.

"Ida, of course, is the more beautiful," continued drunken Dreyer, "but Isolda with that fluffy pale hair and that way of gasping she has while one is telling her something comical—"

"Why don't you sample her? Or both together?"

"I wonder," mused Dreyer as he took off his drawers. He laughed and added: "My love, what about you tonight? After all, it is Christmas."

"Not after your idiotic joke," said Martha, "and if you pester me with your lust I'll take my pillow to the guest room."

"I wonder," repeated Dreyer as he got into bed and laughed again. He had never tried them together. Might be fun! Separately he had had them only on two occasions: Ida three summers ago quite unexpectedly in the woods of Spandau during a picnic; and Isolda a little later in a Dresden hotel. Hopelessly bad stenographers, both of them.

Franz had never gone to bed yet at half past four in the morning. He woke up in the afternoon feeling hungry, healthy, and happy. He remembered with pleasure snatching that mask off. The roaring darkness that had pursued him like a nightmare had been transformed, now that he had surrendered himself to it, into a hum of euphoria.

He dined at the nearby tavern and went back home to wait for Martha. At ten minutes past seven she had not come. At twenty minutes to eight he knew she was not coming. Should he wait till tomorrow? He dared not ring her up: Martha had forbidden him and herself to telephone lest it became a sweet habit which in its turn might lead to the wrong ears' overhearing a careless caressive phrase. The urge to tell her how strong and well he felt, despite all that wine and venison, and music, and terror, was even stronger than his desire to know if her cold was better.

As he reached their street, an empty taxi overtook him and pulled up at the villa. He decided his visit was ill-timed— they were probably going out. He paused at the fence of the garden expecting them to emerge, she in her lovely furs, he in his camelhair coat. Then, changing his mind again, Franz hurried toward the porch.

The front door was ajar. Frieda was pulling half-strangled Tom upstairs by his collar. In the entrance hall Franz saw an opulent suitcase of real leather and a splendid pair of hickory skis of a type they did not have at the store. In the parlor husband and wife stood facing each other. He was talking rapidly, and she was smiling like an angel and nodding in silence.

"Ah, Franz, there you are," he said, turning, and caught his nephew by his stuffed shoulder. "You've come just at the right moment. I'm off for three weeks or so."

"What are those skis doing there?" asked Franz, and realized with surprise that Dreyer had ceased to frighten him.

"Mine. I'm going to Davos. And take this" (five dollars).

He kissed his wife on the cheek. "Nurse your cold, dear. Have a good time over the holidays. Tell Franz to take you to the theater. Don't be cross with me, darling, for leaving you behind. Snow is for men and single girls. You can't change that."

"You'll be late for your train," said Martha, slitting sweet eyes at him.

He glanced at his golden watch, mimicked panic, and grasped his valise. The taxi driver helped with the skis. Uncle, aunt and nephew crossed the garden. After all that frost a drizzle had set in! Hatless and wearing her moleskin coat, Martha strolled to the wicket with an indolent swing of the hips, her hands invisibly clasped in her joined coat-sleeves. It took quite a long time to arrange the long skis on the roof of the taxi. At last the door slammed. The taxi drove off. Franz mechanically noted its license number: 22221. This unexpected "1" seemed odd after so many "2"s. They walked slowly back toward the house along the crunching path.

"It's thawing again," said Martha. "Today my cough is much less harsh."

Franz thought for a moment and said: "Yes. But there are still some cold days ahead."

"Possibly," said Martha.

When they entered the empty house, Franz had the impression they had returned from a funeral.

8

She began teaching him obstinately and fervidly.

After the first embarrassments, stumblings, and perplexities, he gradually began to understand what she was communicating to him, doing so with almost no words of explanation, almost entirely through pantomime. He gave his full attention both to her and to the ululating sound which, now rising, now falling, accompanied him constantly; and already he perceived, in that sound, rhythmic demands, a compelling meaning, regular breaks and beats. What Martha wanted of him was proving to be so simple. As soon as he had assimilated something, she would nod silently, looking down the while with an intent smile, as though following the motions and growth of an already distinct shadow. His awkwardness, that feeling of having a limp and a hump, which tormented him in the beginning—all this soon disappeared; instead, the erect poise, the specious grace and pace she was teaching him enslaved him totally: now he could no longer disobey the sound whose mystery he had solved. Vertigo became a habitual and pleasurable state, an automaton's somnambulic languor, the law of his existence; now Martha would gently exult, and press her temple against his, knowing that they were at one, that he would do the proper thing. While teaching him she restrained her impatience, the impatience he had once noticed in the flash and flicker of her elegant legs. Now she stood before him and, holding up her pleated skirt between finger and thumb, she repeated the steps in slow motion so that he might see for himself the magnified turn of toe and heel. He would attempt a scooping caress but she would slap his hand away and go on with the lesson. And when, under the pressure of her strong palm, he learned how to turn and spin; when his steps had finally fallen in with hers; when a glance at the mirror told her that the clumsy lesson had become a harmonious dance; then she increased the pace, gave her excitement its head, and her rapid cries expressed fierce satisfaction with his obedient piston slide.

He came to know the reeling expanse of parquetry in huge halls surrounded by loges; he leaned his elbow on the faded plush of their parapet; he wiped her powder off his shoulder; he saw himself and her in surfeited mirrors; he paid predatory waiters out of her black silk purse; his mackintosh and her beloved moleskin coat embraced for hours on end in the darkness of heavily laden hangers under the guard of sleepy cloakroom girls; and the sonorous names of all the fashionable ballrooms and dancing cafés—tropical, crystal, royal—became as familiar to him as the names of the streets of the little town where he had dwelt in a previous life. And presently they would be sitting out the next dance, still panting from amorous exertions, side by side on the drab couch in his dingy room.

"Happy New Year," said Martha, "our year. Write to your mother, whom I certainly would like to know, that you are having a splendid time. Think how surprised she will be later . . . afterwards . . . when I shall meet her."

He asked: "When? Have you fixed a deadline?"

"As soon as possible. The sooner the better."

"Oh, we mustn't dawdle."

She leaned back on the cushions, her hands behind her head. "A month—perhaps two. We have to plan very carefully, my dear love."

"I'd go mad without you," said Franz. "Everything upsets me—this wallpaper, the people in the street, my landlord. His wife never shows herself. It's so strange."

"You must be calmer. Otherwise nothing will work out. Come here. . . ."

"I know it will turn out wonderfully," he said, pressing against her. "Only we must make sure of everything. The smallest mistake. . . ."

"Oh, how can you doubt, my strong, stout Franz!"

"No, of course not. God, no. Oh, my God, no. It's just that we have to find a sure method."

"Fast, darling, much faster—don't you hear the rhythm? . . ."

They were no longer coupling on the couch but foxtrotting among gleaming white tables on the bright-lit floor of a café. The orchestra was playing and gasping for breath. There was among the dancers a tall American Negro who smiled tolerantly as one passionate pair bumped into him and his blonde partner.

"We'll find it, we must find it," continued Martha in a rapid patter in time to the music; "after all, we are within our rights."

He saw her long sweet burning eye, and the geranium lobe of her little ear from beneath her sleek bandeau. If only he could glide thus forever, an eternal piston rod in a vacuum of delight, and never, never part from her. . . . But there still existed the store, where he bowed and turned like a jolly doll, and there still were the nights when like a dead doll he lay supine on his bed not knowing whether he was asleep or awake, and who was that, shuffling and two-stepping, and whispering in the corridor, and why was the alarm clock jazzing in his ear? But let us say we are awake, and here comes bushy-browed old Enricht bringing two cups of coffee—why two? And how depressing those torn silk socks on the floor.

One such blurry morning, a Sunday, when he and Martha in her beige dress were walking decorously about the snow-powdered garden, she wordlessly showed him a snapshot she had just received from Davos. It showed a smiling Dreyer, in a Scandinavian ski suit, clutching his poles; his skis were beautifully parallel, and all around was bright snow, and on the snow one could distinguish the photographer's narrow-shouldered shadow.

When the photographer (a fellow-skier and teacher of English, Mr. Vivian Badlook) had clicked the shutter and straightened up, Dreyer, still beaming, moved his left ski forward; however, as he was standing on a slight incline, the ski went further than he had intended, and with a great flourish of ski poles he tumbled heavily on his back while both girls shot past shrieking with laughter. For a while he could not get the damned skis uncrossed, and his arm kept going into the snow up to the elbow. By the time he got up, disfigured by the snow, and put on his snow-crusted mittens, and cautiously began to glide down, his face bore a solemn expression. He had dreamed of performing all kinds of Christianias and telemarks, flying downhill, turning sharply in a cloud of snow—but apparently God had not willed it. In the snapshot, though, he looked like a real skier, and he admired it before slipping it into the envelope. But that morning as he stood by the window in his yellow pajamas and looked at the green larches and the cobalt sky he reflected that he had been there two weeks, and yet his skiing and his English were even worse than the previous winter. From the snow-blue road came the jingle of sleighbells; Isolda and Ida were giggling in the bathroom; but enough was enough. He remembered with a pang of pleasure the inventor, who must already be at work in the laboratory set up for him; he also remembered a number of other entertaining projects connected with the expansion of the Dandy store; he pondered all this, took a look at the snowy slope crisscrossed with shiny ski tracks, and decided to depart for home ahead of time leaving his girl friends to their own devices, which were not negligible; and there was another amusing thought that he deliberately kept in the back of his mind: it would be fun to come home unexpectedly, and catch Martha's soul unawares, and see whether she would let escape a radiant smile of surprise or meet him with her usual ironic morosity as she certainly would if warned of his arrival. Despite his keen sense of humor, Dreyer was too naively self-centered to realize how thoroughly those sudden returns had been exploited in ribald tales.

Franz ripped the photo into little bits which the wind carried across the wet lawn.

"Silly," said Martha, "why did you do that? He's sure to ask me if I pasted it in the album."

"Some day I'll tear up the album too," said Franz.

An eager Tom had come running toward them: he hoped Franz might have thrown a ball or a pebble but a rapid search revealed nothing.

A couple of days later Frieda was allowed to spend the weekend with the family of her brother, a fireman in Potsdam and the brightest Rembrandtesque gleam in her gloomy light. Tom was compelled to spend more time than usual in the gardener's quarters next to the carless garage. Martha and Franz, yielding to the agonizing desire to assert themselves, to be free, to enjoy their freedom, decided, if only for one evening, to live as they craved to live: it was to be a dress rehearsal of future happiness.

"Today you are master here," she said. "Here's your study, here's your armchair, here if you want is the paper: the market has rallied."

He flung off his jacket and sauntered through all the rooms as if reviewing them upon returning to his own comfortable house from a long and difficult journey.

"Everything in order? Is my lord happy?"

He put his arm around her shoulder and they stood side by side before the mirror. He was poorly shaven that evening, and instead of a waistcoat had put on a rather casual dark-red sweater; there was something homy and quiet about Martha too. Her recently washed hair did not lie smoothly, and she wore a woollen jumper that was unbecoming but somehow right.

"Mr. and Mrs. Bubendorf. You know, once we were standing like this, and I was sure you'd kiss me for the first time, but you didn't."

"I'm now an inch taller," he said with a laugh. "Look, we are almost the same height."

He sank into the leather armchair, and she sat in his lap, and the fact that she had gained weight and was quite bottom-heavy made things all the more cozy.

"I love your ear," he said, lifting up a strand of hair with a nose-wrinkling horse-nuzzle.

A clock began chiming gently and tunefully in the next room. Franz laughed softly.

"Imagine if he were suddenly to come in now—just like that."

"Who?" asked Martha. "I don't understand whom you're speaking about."

"I mean him. If he should come home all at once. He has such a stealthy way of opening doors."

"Oh, you are speaking of my late husband, oh, I see," said Martha in a smoky voice. "No, my deceased was always a man of precision. He would let me know—no, no, Franz, not now, after supper, perhaps. I think he meant to be an example to his little wife, who otherwise might visit him— I said no—without warning in that little room with the couch he has at the back of his office."

Silence. Matrimonial well-being.

"The deceased," chuckled Franz, "the deceased."

"Do you remember him well?" murmured Martha, rubbing her nose against his neck.

"Vaguely. And you?"

"The red fur on his belly and—"

In atrocious, disparaging and quite inaccurate terms she described the dead man's private parts.

"Pah," said Franz. "Don't make me throw up."

"Franz," she said, her eyes beaming, "no one will ever find out!"

Well accustomed by now to the idea, by now quite tame and bloodthirsty, he nodded in silence. A certain numbness was invading his lower limbs.

"We did it so simply, so neatly," said Martha, slitting her eyes as if in dim recollection, "not the merest shadow of suspicion. Nothing. And why, sir? Because destiny is on our side. It could not have been otherwise. Remember the funeral? Piffke's tulips? Isolda's and Ida's violets bought from a street beggar?"

He mutely acquiesced again.

"It was during the final thaw. We had forsythias in the

bay window. Remember? I was still coughing but it was already a soft wet delicious cough. Ah, getting rid of the last thick gob."

Franz winced. Another pause.

"You know, my knees are getting sort of tired. No, wait, don't get up. Just move over a little. That's right."

"My treasure, my all," she cried, "my darling husband. I never imagined there could be such a marriage as ours."

He passed his lips along her warm neck and said:

"Isn't it time for us to lie down for a bit, eh?"

"What about some cold cuts and beer? No? Okay, we shall eat afterwards."

She rose, leaning hard on him as she did so. Then she stretched herself.

"Let's go up," she said with a contented yawn, "to our bedroom."

"Is that all right?" asked Franz. "I thought we'd do it here."

"Of course not. Oh, come on, get up. It's already past ten."

"You know. . . . I'm still a little scared of the deceased," said Franz, biting his lip.

"Oh, he won't be coming for a week yet. That's as sure as death. What's there to be scared of? Little fool! Or don't you want me?"

"Oh, I do," said Franz, "but you must cover his bed; I don't want to see it. It would put me off."

She turned off the lights in the parlor and he followed her up an inner staircase that was short and creaky; then they passed through a baby-blue corridor.

"Why on earth are you walking on tiptoe?" exclaimed Martha with a loud laugh. "Can't you understand—we're married, married!"

She showed him the mangle room which she used for her Hindu-kitsch exercises, her dressing room, his and her bathroom, and finally their bedroom.

"The deceased used to sleep on that bed there," she said. "But of course the sheets have been changed. Let me put this tiger rug over it. So. Would you like to wash or something?"

"No, I'll wait for you here," said Franz, examining a soft doll on the night table.

"All right. Undress quick and hop into my bed. I have a great need."

She left the door ajar. Her pleated skirt and jumper were already lying on a chair. From the toilet across the corridor came the steady thick rapid sound of his sister making water. It stopped. Martha passed into the bathroom.

He suddenly felt that in this cold, inimical, unbearably white room where everything reminded him of the dead man, he was unable to undress, let alone make love. With revulsion and fear he gazed at the next bed.

Then he strained his ears. He thought he heard a door slam downstairs followed by creeping steps. He darted to the corridor. Simultaneously Martha came out of the bathroom stark naked.

"Something's happened," he said in a spitting whisper. "We're not alone any more. Listen to that noise."

Martha frowned. Wrapping herself in a negligee, she went down the corridor and stopped with her head bent sidewise.

"I'm telling you! . . . I've heard."

"I too had a bizarre feeling," said Martha in a low voice. "I know, darling, you are terribly disappointed, but we'd better not go on with this madness. It won't be long now. You'd better go. I'll come tomorrow as usual."

"But if I meet somebody downstairs?"

"There's no one there, Franz. Here, take my keys. You'll return them tomorrow."

She accompanied him as far as the main staircase, still listening. Now she was as puzzled and upset as he.

Oh! Down in the hall harsh bangs resounded. Franz stopped, clutching at the banister, but she gave a laugh of relief.

"I know what it is," she said. "That's the downstairs toilet. It sometimes bangs at night if there is a big wind, and if you don't close it well."

"I'll admit I was a little frightened," said Franz.

"All the same, you'd better go, darling. We mustn't take risks. Close that door in passing, will you."

He embraced her. She let herself be kissed on the bare shoulder, drawing back herself the lace of her negligee to grant him that farewell treat. She remained standing on the landing of the theatrically illumined blue staircase until with a winky-winky he was gone.

A strong clean wind hit him in the face. The gravel path crunched pleasantly and securely beneath his feet. Franz inhaled deeply; then he cursed. She was so sinful and beautiful! He felt a man again. Why was he such a coward? To think that a specter, a cadaver, had turned him out of the house where he, Franz, was the real master! Muttering as he went (something that happened to him rather often of late), he walked swiftly along the dark sidewalk, and then without looking right or left began diagonally crossing the street at the place where he always crossed it on his way home.

A taxicab's horn, nasal and nasty, made him jump back. Still muttering, Franz turned the corner. Meanwhile the taxi braked and uncertainly pulled up to the curb. The driver got out and opened the door. "What number, did you say?" he asked. No answer. The driver, reaching into the darkness, shook his fare by the shoulder. Finally the latter opened his eyes, leaned forward. "Number five," he replied to the driver's question. "You're a little off."

The bedroom window glowed. Martha was arranging her hair for the night. Suddenly she froze, still with raised elbows. Now she heard quite distinctly a loud clatter as if something had fallen. She darted toward the stairs. From the front hall came peels of laughter—familiar laughter, alas. He was laughing because, having turned awkwardly with the long skis on his shoulder, he had dropped one of them while knocking off with the other the white brush which flew up like a bird from the looking-glass shelf, after which he had tripped over his own suitcase.

"I am the voyageur," he cried in his best English. *"I half returned from shee-ing!"*

The next instant he knew perfect happiness. There was a magnificent smile on Martha's face. Oh, no doubt, he was pretty to look at, tanned, trimmed by gravity, shedder of at least five pounds (as if Martha and Franz had already started to demolish him), but she was looking not at him: she was looking somewhere over his head, welcoming not him, but wise fate that had so simply and honestly averted a crude, ridiculous, dreadfully overworked disaster.

"A miracle saved us," she later told Franz (for people talk very lightly of miracles), "but let this be a lesson. You can see for yourself: it's impossible to wait any longer. Lucky once, lucky twice, and then—caught. And what can we expect then? Let us suppose he gives me a divorce. Let us even suppose I catch him with a stenographer. He does not have to support me, if I remarry. What next? I'm just as poor as you. My relatives in Hamburg are not going to help me."

Franz shrugged.

"I wonder if you understand," she said, "that his widow inherits a fortune."

"Why do you tell me this? We have discussed it sufficiently. I know perfectly well that there's only one solution."

Then, as she peered through the slippery glint of his glasses deep into the mire of his greenish eyes, she knew that she had achieved her end, that he had been fully prepared, was completely ripe, and that the time had come to act. She was right. Franz no longer had a will of his own; the best he could do was to refract her will in his own way. The easy fulfillment of two merged dreams had become familiar to him, owing to a very simple interplay of sensations. By now Dreyer had already been several times murdered and buried. Not a future happiness, but a future recollection had been rehearsed on a bare stage, before a dark and empty house. With stunning unexpectedness, the corpse had returned out of nowhere, had walked in like an animated snowman, had begun talking as if he were alive. But what of it? It would be easy now and not at all frightening to cope with this sham existence, to make the corpse a corpse once more, and this time for good.

The discussion of methods of murder became with them an everyday matter. No uneasiness, no shame accompanied it; neither did they experience the dark thrill gamblers know, or the comfortable horror a family man enjoys when reading about the destruction of another family, with gory details, in a family newspaper. The words "bullet" and "poison" began to sound about as normal as "bouillon" or "pullet," as ordinary as a doctor's bill or pill. The process of killing a man could be considered as calmly as the recipes in a cookbook, and no doubt Martha first of all thought of poison because of a woman's innate domestic bent, an instinctive knowledge of spices and herbs, of the healthful and the harmful.

From a second-rate encyclopedia they learned about all sorts of dismal Lucrezias and Locustas. A hollow-diamond ring, filled with rainbow venom, tormented Franz's imagination. He would dream at night of a treacherous handshake. Half-awake, he would recoil and not dare to move: somewhere under him, on the sheet, the prickly ring had just rolled, and he was terrified it might sting him. But in the daytime, by Martha's serene light, all was simple again. Tofana, a Sicilian girl, who dispatched 639 people, sold her "aqua" in vials mislabelled with the innocent image of a saint. The Earl of Leicester had a mellower method: his victim would blissfully sneeze after a pinch of lethal snuff. Martha would impatiently shut the P-R volume and search in another. They learned, with complete indifference, that toxemia caused anemia and that Roman law saw in deliberate toxication a blend of murder and betrayal. "Deep thinkers," remarked Martha with a snarling laugh, sharply turning the page. Still she could not get to the heart of the matter. A sardonic "See" sent her to something called "alkaloids." Another "See" led to the fang of a centipede, magnified, if you please. Franz, unaccustomed to big encyclopedias, breathed heavily as he looked over her shoulder. Climbing through the barbed wire of formulae, they read for a long time about the uses of morphine, until having reached in some tortuous way a special case of pneumonia cruposa, Martha suddenly understood that the toxin in question belonged to a domesticated variety. Turning to another letter, they discovered that strychnine caused spasms in frogs and laughing fits in some islanders. Martha was beginning to fume. She kept brutally yanking out the thick tomes and squeezing them back any which way in the bookcase. There were fleeting glimpses of colored plates: military decorations, Etruscan vases, gaudy butterflies. . . . "Here, this is more like it," said Martha, and she read in a low solemn voice: "vomiting, a feeling of dejection, a singing in the ears —don't wheeze like that, please—a sensation of itching and burning over the entire surface of the skin, the pupils narrowed to the size of a pinhead, the testicles become like oranges. . . ." Franz remembered how as an adolescent he had looked up "onanism" in a much smaller encyclopedia at school, and remained terrified and chaste for almost a week.

"Chucks," said Martha, "that's all medical rot. Who wants to know about cures or about traces of arsenic found in a stinking dead ass. I suppose we need some special works. There is a treatise mentioned here in parentheses, but it is a work written in the sixteenth century in Latin. Why people should use Latin is beyond me. Pull yourself together, Franz —he's here."

She unhurriedly put the volume back and unhurriedly closed the glass doors of the cabinet. From the ancient world of the dead came Dreyer, whistling as he approached with the bouncing dog. But she did not give up the idea of poison. In the morning, alone, she again scanned the evasive articles in the encyclopedia, trying to find that plain, unhistorical, unspectacular, matter-of-fact potion or powder that she so clearly imagined. By accident at the end of one paragraph, she came upon a brief bibliography of plausible-looking modern works. She sought Franz's advice as to whether they ought to obtain one of them. He gave her a blank look but said that if it were necessary he would go and buy it. But she was afraid to let him go alone. They might tell him that the book had to be ordered or it would turn out to consist of ten volumes costing twenty-five marks each. He might get flustered, foolishly leave his address. If she were to accompany way, you haven't told me of your own summer plans. I've heard of a fellow who could not remember a funny story and burst a blood vessel."

"It's not the fact that I can't remember it that hurts," Dreyer said plaintively. "What hurts is that I'll remember it the minute we part. No, we haven't decided yet. Isn't that so, my love? We haven't decided yet? In fact" (turning to Willy), "we haven't discussed it at all. I know she hates the Alps. Venice means nothing to her. It's all very difficult. There was a twist at the end, such an amusing one. . . ."

"Drop it, drop it," puffed Willy. "How come you haven't decided yet? It's the end of June. High time."

"Perhaps," said Dreyer with a quizzical glance at his wife, "perhaps we might go to the seaside."

"Water," nodded Willy. "Lots of blue water. That's good. So would I, with delight. But I'm being dragged off to Paris. I am a remarkably good diver, though you wouldn't believe it."

"I can't even swim," glumly answered Dreyer. "I'm no good at some sports. Same thing with skiing. I seem always to stay at the same point: the swing, the knack, the equipoise, just aren't there. I'm not sure those new skis were the right ones for me. My love, I know you hate the seaside but let's go there once more. We'll take Franz and Tom with us. We'll splash and puddle. And you'll go boating with Franz, and get as brown as milk chocolate."

And Martha smiled. Not that she realized whence came that breath of moist freshness. The magic lantern of fancy slipped a colored slide in—a long sandy beach on the Baltic where they had once been in 1924, a white pier, bright flags, striped booths, a thousand striped booths—and now they were thinning, they broke off, and beyond for many miles

westward stretched the empty whiteness of the sands between heather and water. Water. What do you do to ex-
tinguish a fire? An infant could tell you that.

"We'll go to Gravitz," she said, turning to Willy.

She grew unusually animated. Her glossy lips parted. Her
elongated eyes flashed like jewels. Two sickle-shaped dim-
ples appeared on her flaming cheeks. Excitedly she began
telling Elsa Wald about a little dressmaker (they are always
"little") whom she had discovered. And ecstatically she
praised Elsa's perfume. Dreyer, eating strawberries, watched
her and rejoiced. She had simply never beamed and babbled
so prettily when visiting the Walds ("they are your friends,
not mine").

"We'll have to have a serious talk," she said on the way
home. "Sometimes you do get good ideas. Look, tomorrow
morning you write and reserve two adjacent rooms and a
single one at the Seaview Hotel. But the dog we'll leave—it
would only be a bother. You'd better make haste or there'll
be no rooms left."

Being a little drunk, he glued himself to her warm nape.
She pushed him away quite good-naturedly and said:

"I see you're not only a lecher but also a liar."

He suddenly looked worried. "What do you mean?"

"I thought," she said, "you told me—when was that? A
year ago?—that you were taking lessons at the Freibad, and
that you now swam like a fish."

"An inexcusable exaggeration," he answered, much relieved. "A very poor fish, really. I keep afloat for three
meters, and then I sink like a log."

"Except that logs don't sink," said Martha merrily.

Make haste! But now haste was lighthearted. With waves
and sunlight all around, how easy to breathe, to kill, to love.
The single word "water" had resolved everything. Although

Martha knew nothing about mathematical problems and the pleasure of elegant proof, she recognized the solution of her problem at once by its simplicity and limpidity. This harmonious obviousness, this elementary grace made her ashamed—as well she might be—of her gropings and clumsy fancies. She felt an inordinate desire to see Franz that very minute, or at least to do something—to cable him the code word at once, but for the time being the message ran MIDNIGHT TAXI STOP RAIN GATE FRONT HALL STAIRS BEDROOM PLEASE STOP ALL RIGHT HURRY UP GOOD NIGHT. And tomorrow was Sunday—how do you like that! She had warned Franz that if the weather did not improve she would not go to see him because Dreyer would not be playing tennis. But even this delay, which once would have driven her into a rage, now seemed trifling in the light of her newfound confidence.

She woke up a little later than usual, and her first sensation was that the night before something exquisite had happened. On the terrace Dreyer had finished his coffee and was reading the newspaper. When she came down, radiant, wearing pale-green crepe, he rose and kissed her cool hand as he always did at their Sunday morning meetings, but this time he added to it a good-natured twinkle of gratitude. The silver sugar bowl blazed blindingly in the sun, dimmed slowly, and flamed forth again.

"Can the courts still be wet?" said Martha.

"I've telephoned," he answered, and went back to his paper. "They are soaked. An archeologist has found a tomb in Egypt with toys and blue thistles three thousand years old."

"Thistles are not blue," said Martha, reaching for the coffee pot. "Have you written about the rooms?"

He nodded without raising his eyes and went on nodding

even more gently as he read his paper, cheerfully reminding himself between the nods and the lines to dictate it tomorrow at the office.

Oh, keep nodding . . . keep playing the fool . . . it does not matter now. He's a first-rate swimmer—that's not tennis for you! She, too, was born on the banks of a big river, and could stay afloat for hours, for days, forever.

She used to lie on her back, and the water would lap and rock her, so delicious, so cool. And the bracing breeze penetrating you as you sat naked with a naked boy of your age among the forget-me-nots. These thoughts came without effort. She need not invent, she had only to develop what was already there in outline. How happy her darling would be! Should she ring him up and say only one word: *Wasser?*

Dreyer noisily folded his paper as if wrapping a bird in it and said: "Let's go and have a walk, eh? What do you say?"

"You go," she replied. "I have to write some letters. We must head off Hilda, you know."

He thought: what if I ask her, tenderly, tenderly. It's a free morning. We are lovers again.

But emotional energy had never been his forte, and he said nothing.

A minute later, Martha, from the terrace, saw him walk to the gate with his raincoat over his arm, open the wicket, let Tom pass first like a lady, and saunter off, lighting up a cigar as he went.

She sat motionless. The sugar bowl alternately blazed and dimmed. All at once a gray little spot appeared on the tablecloth; then another beside it. A drop fell on her hand. She rose, looking up. Frieda began hurriedly clearing away the dishes and the tablecloth, also glancing now and then at the sky. Thunder rumbled, and an astonished sparrow landed on the balustrade—and darted away. Martha went into the house. The door of the hallway toilet was banging. Frieda, already half-drenched, with the tablecloth in her embrace, laughing and muttering to herself, rushed from the terrace kitchenward. Martha stood at the center of the oddly dark parlor. Now everything outside was gurgling, murmuring, breathing. She wondered if she should first ring him up, but her impatience was too strong—the fuss with the telephone would be a waste of time. She put on her mackintosh with a rustling sound and snatched up an umbrella. Frieda brought her hat and handbag from the bedroom. "You ought to wait it out," said Frieda. "It's a regular deluge." Martha laughed and said she had quite forgotten an appointment at a café with Mrs. Bayader and another lady, an expert in rhythmic respiration ("Mixed respiration," Frieda, who knew more than she ought to have known, kept snorting every now and then the whole morning.) The rain began drumming on the taut silk of her umbrella. The wicket swung shut, splashing her hand. She walked quickly along the mirrory sidewalk, hurrying toward the taxi stand. The sun struck the long streams of rain causing them to slant, as it were, and presently they turned golden and mute. Again and again the sun struck, and the shattered rain now flew in single fiery drops, and the asphalt cast reflections of iridescent violet, and everything grew so bright and hot that wet-haired Dreyer shed his raincoat as he walked, and Tom, who was somewhat darker after the rain, perked up and marched on a brown dachshund. Tom and the dachshund circled in one spot, or rather Tom circled while the dackel turned abruptly in one piece every now and then, until Dreyer whistled. He walked slowly, looking right and left, trying to find the newly built cinema that Willy had mentioned the night before. He found himself in a district he had seldom visited although it was not far from his house. He turned into a park to give the dog more exercise and then cut across a piece of wasteland adjoining an unfamiliar boulevard. A little farther he crossed a square and saw at the corner of the next street a tall house bared of most of its scaffolding: its first story was ornamented with a huge picture, advertising the film to be shown on the opening night, July 15, based on Goldemar's play *King, Queen, Knave* which had been such a hit several years ago. The display consisted of three gigantic transparent-looking playing cards resembling stained-glass windows which would probably be very effective when lit up at night: the King wore a maroon dressing gown, the Knave a red turtleneck sweater, and the Queen a black bathing suit. "Must not forget to order those rooms tomorrow," reflected Dreyer, and another important note that the faithful Miss Reich would write over her signature: Dr. Eier must leave the city and to his great regret cannot continue to pay for the flat where you persist in receiving other idiots, or something along those lines.

He was about to turn back when Tom gave a short muffled bark and Franz came out of a little café wiping his mouth with his knuckles.

"Well, well, well, fancy running into you," exclaimed Dreyer. "Starting the day with a schnapps, eh?"

"My landlord has stopped serving me breakfast," said Franz. What a horrible encounter. Side by side they walked, eyed by luminous puddles.

They almost never had occasion to be alone together, and Dreyer now realized that they had absolutely nothing to talk about. It was an odd feeling. He tried to clarify it for himself. He saw Franz practically every other evening at his house but always in Martha's presence; Franz fitted naturally into those usual surroundings, occupying a place long since set aside for him, and Dreyer never spoke to him in any but a joking casual way seeking no information, and expressing no feeling, accepting Franz on trust amid the rest of the familiar objects and people, and interrupting with irrelevant remarks the silly and dull narratives that Franz vaguely directed at Martha. Dreyer was well aware of his own secret shyness, of his inability to have a frank, serious, heart-to-heart talk with a person whom ruthless chance confronted him with. Now he felt both apprehension and an urge to laugh at the silence that was being wedged between him and Franz. He had not the least idea what to do about it. Ask him where he was going? He cleared his throat and gave Franz a sidelong glance. Franz looked at the ground as he walked.

"Where are you going?" asked Dreyer.

"I live near here," said Franz with an indefinite gesture. Dreyer was looking at him not unkindly. Let him look, thought Franz. Everything in life is senseless, and this walk is senseless too.

"Fine, fine," said Dreyer. "I think I've never been here. I cut through a wilderness of kitchen gardens, and then suddenly there were half-built houses all around me. By the way, you know what—why don't you show me your apartment?"

Franz nodded. Silence. Presently he pointed to the right and both involuntarily quickened their step in order to accomplish at least one not wholly aimless act—a right turn. Tom, too, looked ennuied. He was not overfond of Franz.

"How stupid," thought Dreyer. "I must find something to tell him. We are not following a hearse." He wondered if he should not tell him about the electric mannequins. It might interest a young man. The subject in fact was so entertaining that he had to make quite an effort not to gush about it at home. Lately the Inventor had asked him not to visit the workshop, saying he wanted to prepare a surprise, and then the other day, looking very smug, he invited Dreyer to come. The sculptor who looked like a scientist and the professor who looked like an artist also seemed extremely pleased with themselves. Two young men from the store, Moritz and Max, could hardly hide their giggles. Pulling at a cord, the Inventor drew open a black curtain, also an innovation, and a pale dignified gentleman in dinner jacket, with a carnation in his buttonhole, walked out of the side door at the left, crossed the room at a lifelike though somewhat somnambulic gait, and left by the side door at the right. Behind the scenes he was seized by Moritz and Max, who changed his clothes while a youth in white, with a racket under his arm, wandered across the room in his turn and was immediately followed by somnambule number one, now wearing a gray suit with an elegant tie and carrying a briefcase. He dropped it absentmindedly before leaving the stage but Moritz retrieved it and followed him to the exit. Meanwhile the youth reappeared, now sporting a cherry-red blazer, and after him the older man, soberly clad in a raincoat, ambled along in his melancholy and mysterious dream.

Dreyer found the show absolutely entrancing: not only did those grandly trousered legs and properly shod feet move with a stylized grace that no mechanical toy had ever achieved before, but the two faces were fashioned with exquisite care in the same wax-like substance as the hands. And when vulgar young Max humorously impersonated the younger automannequin by stalking and prancing in his wake on the delightful youth's final appearance, none could doubt which of the two personages had more human charm, though one Inventor was so much more experienced than the other. Presently the mature gentleman came by for the last time, and at this point his creator had devised matters in such a way as to have the re-tuxedoed one (minus the carnation mislaid in some avatar) stop in mid-stage, jiggle his feet a little as if demonstrating a dance step, and then continue toward the exit with his arm crooked as if escorting an invisible lady. "Next time," said the Inventor, "a woman will be added. Beauty is easy to render because beauty is based on the rendering of beauty, but we are still working on her hips, we want her to roll them, and that is difficult."

But could one describe all this to Franz? Told in a jocular tone it would be of no interest, and if made serious, Franz might not believe it since Dreyer had pulled his leg too frequently in the past. All at once a saving thought flashed through his mind. Franz did not know yet that he was being invited to the seaside and of course should be told the good news; and simultaneously Dreyer recalled the end of the anecdote that had eluded him on the eve. First, though, he told him about the trip, saving the anecdote for the last. Franz mumbled that he was very grateful. Dreyer explained to him what to buy for the trip, charging everything to Uncle, *selbstverständlich!* Franz, reviving a little, thanked him again more eloquently.

"Are you thinking of marriage?" asked Dreyer (Franz made the gesture of a clown's stooge when presented with a conundrum). "Because I might find you a very amorous bride."

Franz grinned. "I'm too poor," he replied. "Perhaps if I got a raise."

"That's an idea," said Dreyer.

"We are almost there," said Franz, and almost fell over Tom, who had stopped.

Dreyer decided he would wait to tell his story—which was really an extremely funny one—until they were in Franz's room: certain vehement gestures and extravagant attitudes had to accompany the story. This was a fatal post-ponement. He never told it. They were now in front of the house where another good anecdote was in the process of what botanically minded folklorists call "exfoliating." Tom stopped again, looking up and then back. "March-march," said Dreyer, and with his knee pushed the intelligent hound.

"I live there," said Franz pointing at the fifth floor.

"Well, let's go in by all means," said Dreyer, and held the door open for Tom, who shot upstairs with a whimper of excitement.

"Good Lord, I must get him some other quarters. No nephew of mine should live in a slum," reflected Dreyer, as he climbed the stairs whose meager carpeting disappeared at an elevation well below timberline. While they climbed Martha had time to finish darning a last hole. She was sitting on the dear decrepit couch leaning over her work, her lips puckering and moving in a happy domestic pout. The land-lord had said that Franz would be back in a moment. He had popped out to eat a bigger breakfast than a sick old woman could prepare. Martha got up to return the socks to their drawer. She was already wearing the emblematic slip-pers and had laid out the little rubber basin coquettishly covered with a clean towel. She stopped in a half-bent atti-tude holding her breath. "He's here," she thought and gave a blissful sigh. Then a strange patter of nonhuman footfalls came along the corridor; a horribly familiar bark rang out. "Quiet, Tom, behave yourself," said Dreyer's cheerful voice. "Third door on your right," said Franz's voice. Martha made for the door in order to turn the key in the lock. The key was on the other side. "Here?" asked Dreyer, and the handle moved. She braced her whole body against the door, holding the handle with her strong hand. The key was heard to turn this way and that. Tom was ardently sniffing under the door.

The handle attempted to jerk again. There were now two men against her. She slipped and lost a slipper, which had happened already in another life. "What's the matter?" said Dreyer's voice. "Your door doesn't open." Her efficient lover was helping to press on the door. "Two idiots," thought Martha coldly, and started to slide again. She heaved with her shoulder and forced it shut. Franz was muttering: "I don't understand it at all. Maybe it's some joke of my landlord's." Tom was barking his head off. He shall be destroyed tomorrow. Dreyer was chuckling and advising Franz to call the police. "Let's kick it in," he said. Martha felt she could not hold the door any longer. Suddenly there was silence, and in the silence a squeaky querulous voice uttered the magic anti-sesame: "Your girl is in there."

Dreyer turned. An old man in a dressing gown, clutching a kettle, was shaking his shaggy gray head at the young imbecile who had covered his face with his hands. Tom was sniffing at the old man. Dreyer burst out laughing and, dragging the dog by the collar, started to walk away. Franz accompanied him to the hallway, and tripped over a pail. "Aha, that's what you're up to," said Dreyer. He winked, nudged Franz in the solar plexus, and went out. Tom looked back—and then followed his master. Franz, wooden-faced and a bit unsteady on his feet, returned along the corridor and opened the now unresisting door. Rosy, dishevelled, panting, as though after a fight, Martha was looking for her slippers.

Impetuously she embraced Franz. Beaming and laughing, she kissed him on the lips, on the nose, on his spectacles, then sat him down beside her on the bed, gave him a drink of water, he rocked limply, and dropped his head in her lap; she stroked his hair and softly, soothingly, explained to him the only, the liquid, the resplendent solution.

She was home before her husband, and when he arrived, and Tom trotted up to her, she gave the dog a withering derisive look.

"Listen," said Dreyer, "our little Franz—no, just imagine—" he spluttered and shook his head for a long time until he finally told her. The image of his somber and awkward nephew fondling a big, hefty sweetheart was unspeakably comic. He recalled Franz hopping on one foot in soiled underpants and his mirth increased. "I think you're simply envious," said Martha, and he tried to hug her.

The very next time Franz came to supper his clever uncle began poking fun at him. Martha kicked her husband under the table. "My dear Franz," said Dreyer, moving out of her shoe's range, "perhaps you don't feel like going away to a distant shore, perhaps you are perfectly happy in town. You can speak frankly. After all I was young myself."

Or else he would turn to Martha and casually observe: "You know, I've hired a private detective. His job is to see that my clerks lead an ascetic life, do not drink, do not gamble, and especially do not—" Here he pressed his fingers to his lips as if he had said too much, and glanced at his victim. "Of course I'm joking," he continued in mock confusion, and added in a thin artificial voice, as if changing the subject: "What lovely weather we're having."

Only a few days remained before the scheduled departure. Martha was so happy, so calm, that nothing could now affect her very deeply: her husband's witticisms would soon end as would everything else—his cigar, his eau de cologne, his shadow with the shadow of a book on the white terrace. One thing only—the fact that the director of the Seaview Hotel had had the impudence to take advantage of the vacational influx and demand a colossal price for the rooms—only this could still perturb her. It was certainly a pity that

Dreyer's removal would be so expensive—especially now, when they had to save every penny because before you knew it he could in those last few days lose, she said, his entire fortune. Some grounds for such apprehension did exist. But at the same time she experienced a certain odd satisfaction at the thought that now, at the very moment when he was to die under her supervision, Dreyer seemed to have exhausted the brilliant business imagination, the gift of daring enterprise, thanks to which he had prepared a fortune to leave to his not ungrateful widow.

She did not know that paradoxically, at that period of decline and indolence, Dreyer had quietly started on the very expensive affair of the automannequins. Question: Were they not too glamorous, too extravagant, too original and luxurious, for the needs of a stodgy bourgeois store in Berlin? On the other hand, he did not doubt one minute that the invention would fetch a spectacular price if one could dazzle and enchant the prospective buyer. Mr. Ritter, an American businessman who had the knack of making fancy stuff work for him, was soon to arrive. I'll sell it, reflected Dreyer. Wouldn't mind selling the whole store as well.

Secretly he realized that he was a businessman by accident and that *his* fantasies were not salable. His father had wanted to be an actor, had been a make-up man in a travelling circus, had tried to design theatrical scenery, wonderful velvet costumes, and had ended as a moderately successful tailor. In his boyhood Kurt had wanted to be an artist—any kind of artist—but instead had spent many dull years working in his father's shop. The greatest artistic satisfaction he ever derived was from his commercial ventures during the inflation. But he knew quite well that he would appreciate even more other arts, other inventions. What prevented him from seeing the world? He had the means—but there was some fatal veil between him and every dream that beckoned to him. He was a bachelor with a beautiful marble wife, a passionate hobbyist without anything to collect, an explorer not knowing on what mountain to die, a voracious reader of unmemorable books, a happy and healthy failure. Instead of arts and adventures, he meanly contented himself with a suburban villa, with a humdrum vacation at a Baltic resort —and even that thrilled him as the smell of a cheap circus used to intoxicate his gentle bumbling father.

That little trip to Pomerania Bay was in fact proving to be quite a boon for everybody concerned, including the god of chance (Cazelty or Sluch, or whatever his real name was), once you imagined that god in the role of a novelist or a playwright, as Goldemar had in his most famous work. Martha was getting ready for the seaside with systematic and blissful zest. Lying on Franz's breast, sprawling all over him, strong and heavy, and a little sticky from the heat, she whispered into his mouth and ear that his torments would be soon allayed. She purchased—not at her husband's store— oh, no—various festive fripperies, a black bathing suit, a beachrobe zigzagged with blue and green, flannel slacks, a new camera, and a lot of bright clothes, which, she chided herself with a smile, was reckless since she would be so soon in mourning. Dreyer depended on the emporium for a tremendous beach ball and a new type of water wings.

She wrote to her sister Hilda, who had tentatively suggested they all spend summer together, that this year plans were uncertain, they might go for a few days to the seaside, or again they might not, she would write if they did and found they wanted to stay longer. She permitted Frieda to remain in the attic but forbade her to receive visitors there. She told the gardener that hysterical Tom had bitten her, that she did not wish to upset her husband, but that she wanted the beast to be put quickly to sleep as soon as they left for Gravitz. The gardener seemed about to demur, but she pushed a fifty-mark note into his honest, caterpillar-stained claw, and the old soldier shrugged his consent.

On the eve of their departure she inspected all the rooms of the villa, furniture, dishes, pictures, whispering to herself and to them that in a very short time she would return, she would return free and happy. That day Franz showed her a letter from his mother. The woman wrote that Emmy would be getting married in a year. "In a year," smiled Martha, "in a year, my darling, another wedding will be taking place too. Come on, cheer up, stop picking your navel. Everything is fine."

They were meeting for the last time in the shabby room which already had an apprehensive unnatural look as happens when a furnished room parts with its tenant forever. Martha had already taken the red slippers home with her and hidden them in a trunk but she did not quite know what to do with the doilies, the two pretty cushions, and the dainty implementa so full of memories. With a heavy heart she advised Franz to wrap it all up and mail it to his sister as a thoughtful wedding present. The little room was aware it was being talked about and was assuming a more and more strained expression. The lewd bidders were appraising the big-nippled bronze-bangled slave girl for the last time. The pattern on the wallpaper—bouquets of blood-brown flowers in a regular succession of repeated variations—arrived at the door from three directions but then there was no further place to go, and they could not leave the room, just as human thoughts, admirably coordinated though they may be, cannot escape the confines of their private circle of hell. Two suitcases stood in a corner, one brand-new in brown leatherette, with its pretty little key still attached to the grip, a sweetheart's gift; the other, a black fibrous affair, bought a year ago at a market stall, and still quite usable except that one lock would sometimes fly open without provocation. All that had been brought into this room, or had accumulated there in the course of ten months, disappeared in those two suitcases which were to depart on the morrow—forever.

That last night Franz did not go out for supper. He closed the empty chest-of-drawers, looked around, opened the window, and seated himself with his feet on the ledge. He must somehow get through this night. The best thing was not to move, not to think, to sit and listen to the far-off automobile horns, to gaze at the blue ink of the sky, at a distant balcony where a lamp glowed under its orange shade, and two happy, innocent, carefree people were playing chess, bent over the bright oasis of the happy table. That third of a man's consciousness, the imaginable future, had ceased to exist for Franz except as a dark cage full of monstrous tomorrows huddled up in an amorphous heap. What had struck Martha as the first realistic, logical solution of all their problems had all but dealt the last blow to his sanity. It would be as she had said—or would it? A flutter of panic brushed his heart. Maybe it was not yet too late. . . . Maybe he should write to his mother, or to his sister and her fiancé to come and take him away. Last Sunday fate had almost saved him, it might save him again, yes—send a telegram home, come down with typhus, or perhaps lean forward a little and slip into the ever-ready embrace of greedy gravity. But the flutter passed. It would be as she had said.

Barefoot, coatless, he sat there a long time hugging his knees without moving, without changing the position of his thighs, even though a knob on the ledge hurt him and a humming mosquito was preparing to strike at his temple. It was by now quite dark in the doomed room, but there was nobody to turn on the light and there would never be anybody if he fell off the sill. On the distant balcony the chess game had long since ended. One by one, or by twos and even threes, all the windows had grown dark. Presently he felt stiff and cold, and slowly clambered back into the room and went to bed. Sometime after midnight the landlord passed noiselessly along the corridor. He checked if there was a slit of light under Franz's door, listened with bent head, and went back to his room. He knew perfectly well that there was no Franz behind the door, that he had created Franz with a few deft dabs of his facile fancy. Yet the jest had to be brought to some natural conclusion. It would be silly to have a figment of one's imagination using up expensive electricity or trying to open a jugular vein with a razor. Besides, old Enricht was getting bored with this particular creature of his. It was time to dispose of him, and replace him with a new one. One sweep of his thought arranged the matter: let this be the fictitious lodger's last night; let him go tomorrow morning—leaving the usual insolent mess as they all do. He postulated, therefore, that tomorrow was the first of the month, that the lodger himself wished to leave—that, in fact, he had paid what he owed. Everything now was in order. Thus, having invented the necessary conclusion, old Enricht, alias Pharsin, dragged up in retrospect and added to it in a lump that which in the past must have led up to this conclusion. For he knew perfectly well—had known for the last eight years at least—that the whole world was but a trick of his, and that all those people—eight former lodgers, doctors, policemen, garbage collectors, Franz, Franz's lady friend, the noisy gentleman with the noisy dog, and even his own, Pharsin's, wife, a quiet little old lady in a lace cap, and he himself, or rather his inner roommate, an elder companion, so to speak, who had been a teacher of mathematics eight years ago, owed their existence to the power of his imagination and suggestion and the dexterity of his hands. In fact, he himself could at any moment turn into a mouse-trap, a mouse, an old couch, a slave girl led away by the highest bidder. Such magicians should be made emperors.

The waking hour struck. With a scream, shielding his head with his arms, Franz leapt off the bed and rushed to the door; there he stopped, trembling, looking around myopically, already aware that nothing special had happened, that it was seven a.m. on a hazy, tender, melting morning with its hullabaloo of sparrows and an express train that was to leave in an hour and a half.

He had slept in his day shirt and had sweated profusely. His clean linen was already packed and anyway it was not worth the trouble of changing. The washstand was bare except for the thin relic of what had been a beige cake of violet-scented soap. He spent a long time scraping up with his fingernail a hair that was stuck to the soap; the hair would assume a different curve but refuse to come off. Dry soap collected under his fingernails. He started to wash his face. That single hair now stuck to his cheek, then to his neck, then tickled his lip. The day before he had packed the land-lord's towel. He paused pondering—and dried himself with a corner of the bed sheet. There was no point in shaving. His hairbrush was packed but he had a pocket comb. His scalp felt scaly and itched. He buttoned up his wrinkled shirt. Never mind. Nothing mattered. Trying to ignore loathsome contacts, he attached his soft collar, which immediately grasped him around the neck like a cold compress. A broken fingernail caught in the silk of his tie. His second-best trousers, which had lain where they had been shed, at the foot of the bed, had gathered some nameless fluff. The clothes brush was packed. The ultimate disaster occurred while he was putting on his shoes: a shoelace broke. He had to suck the tip and ease it into its hole with the result that two short ends were diabolically difficult to make into a knot. Not only animals, but so-called inanimate objects, feared and hated Franz.

At last he was ready. He put on his wristwatch and pocketed the alarm clock. Yes, it was time to leave for the station. He donned his raincoat and hat, responded with a shudder to his reflection in the mirror, picked up the suitcases, and, bumping against the doorjamb as if he were a clumsy passenger in a speeding train, went out into the corridor. The remnants of his physical self that he left behind were a little dirty water at the bottom of the wash basin and a full chamber pot in the middle of the room.

He stopped in the passage, stunned by an unpleasant thought: good manners bade him take leave of old Enricht. He put down the suitcases and knocked hurriedly at the landlord's bedroom door. No answer. He pushed the door and stepped in. The old woman whose face he had never seen sat with her back to him in her usual place. "I'm leaving; I want to say good-by," he said, advancing toward the armchair. There was no old woman at all—only a gray wig stuck on a stick and a knitted shawl. He knocked the whole dusty contraption to the floor. Old Enricht came out from behind a screen. He was stark naked and had a paper fan in his hand. "You no longer exist, Franz Bubendorf," he said dryly, indicating the door with his fan.

Franz bowed and went out without a word. On the stairs he felt dizzy. Setting down his load on a step, he stood clutching the banister. Then he bent over it as over a ship's side and was noisily and hideously sick. Weeping, he collected his valises, re-clicked the reluctant lock. As he proceeded downstairs, he kept meeting various traces of his misadventure. At last the house opened, let him out, and closed again.

12

The main thing of course was the sea: grayish blue, with a blurred horizon, immediately above which a series of cloudlets glided single-file as if along a straight groove, all alike, all in profile. Next came the curve of the bathing beach with its army of striped booth-like shelters, clustering especially densely at the root of the pier which stretched far out amid a flock of rowboats for hire. If one looked from the Seaview Hotel, the best at Gravitz, one could catch now and then one of the booths suddenly leaning forward and crawling over to a new location, like a red-and-white scarab. On the land side of the beach ran a stone promenade, bordered by locust trees on whose black trunks, after the rain, snails would come to life and stick out of their round shells a pair of sensitive yellow little horns that made no less sensitive Franz's flesh creep. Still farther inland came in a row the facades of lesser hotels, pensions, souvenir shops. The balcony of the Dreyers acted the hotel's name. Franz's room sulkily faced a town street parallel to the promenade. Beyond that stretched the second-class hotels, then another parallel lane with the third-class accommodations. The further from the sea the cheaper they grew as if the sea were a stage and they, rows of seats. Their names attempted in one way or another to suggest the sea's presence. Some of them did it with matter-of-fact pride, others preferred metaphors and symbols. Here and there occurred feminine names such as "Aphrodite" to which no boarding house could really live up. There was one villa that either in irony or owing to a topographical error called itself Helvetia. As the distance from the beach increased, the names grew more and more poetical. Then abruptly they gave up and became Central Hotel, Post Hotel, and the inevitable Continental. Hardly anybody hired any of the poor boats near the pier, and no wonder. Dreyer, a wretched sailor, could not imagine how he or any other tourist would care to go out rowing on that desolate expanse of water, when there were so many other things to do at the seaside. For instance? Well, sunbathing; but the sun was a little cruel to the russet of his skin. Sitting around in cafés was not unpleasant although it could be overdone too. There was the Blue Terrace café where the pastry, he thought, was so good. The other day as they were having ice chocolate there, Martha counted at least three foreigners among the crowd. One, judging by his newspaper, was a Dane. The other two were a less easily determinable pair: the girl was trying in vain to attract the attention of the café cat, a small black animal sitting on a chair and licking one hind paw rigidly raised like a shouldered club. Her companion, a suntanned fellow, smoked and smiled. What language were they speaking? Polish? Esthonian? Leaning near them against the wall was some kind of net: a bag of pale-bluish gauze on a ring fixed to a rod of light metal.

"Shrimp catchers," said Martha. "I want shrimps for dinner tonight." (She clicked her front teeth.)

"No," said Franz. "That's not a fisherman's net. That's for catching mosquitoes."

"Butterflies," said Dreyer, lifting an index finger.

"Who wants to catch butterflies?" remarked Martha.

"Oh, it must be good sport," said Dreyer. "In fact, I think to have a passion for something is the greatest happiness on earth."

"Finish your chocolate," said Martha.

"Yes," said Dreyer. "I think it's fascinating, the secrets you find in most ordinary people. That reminds me: Piffke—yes, yes, fat pink Piffke—collects beetles and is a famous expert on them."

"Let's go," said Martha. "Those arrogant foreigners are staring at you."

"Let's go for a good ramble," suggested Dreyer.

"Why don't we hire a boat?" said Martha for a change.

"Count me out," said Dreyer.

"Anyway, let's go somewhere else," said Martha.

As she passed the cat's chair, she tilted it and said "Shoo," and the cat, magically four-legged again, slipped off the seat and vanished.

Dreyer strolled off alone, leaving his wife and nephew on another terrace. This was the second or third tour he was making of the local display windows. Immemorial souvenirs. Picture postcards. The most frequent object of their derision was human obesity and its necessary opposite, Herr and Frau Matchshin of Hungerburg. A monstrous bottom in bathing tights was being pinched by a red crab (resurrected from the boiled), but the nipped lady beamed, thinking it was the hand of an admirer. A red dome above the water was the belly of a fat man floating on his back. There was a "Kiss at Sunset," emblemized by a pair of huge pygal-shaped impressions left on the sand. Skinny, spindle-legged husbands in shorts accompanied pumpkin-bosomed wives. Dreyer was touched by the many photographs going back to the preceding century: the same beach, the same sea, but women in broad-shouldered blouses and men in straw hats. And to think that those over-dressed kiddies were now businessmen, officials, dead soldiers, engravers, engravers' widows.

A sea breeze made the awnings clack. Little bags of pink muslin were crammed with seashells—or was it hard candy? A barometer in the image of a gents' and ladies' lavatory with different sexes emerging according to differences in the weather engaged for a while his awed attention. A second-rate store of men's clothes advertised a liquidation sale. Local seascapists depicted storm-tossed ships, foam-spattered rocks, and the reflection of a yellow moon in an indigo sea. And for no particular reason Dreyer suddenly felt very sad.

Weaving his way among the ramparts of sand that surrounded each bather's ephemeral domain, hurrying to nowhere in order to prove by a great show of haste how much his merchandise was in demand, an itinerant photographer, ignored by the lazy crowd, walked with his camera, yelling into the wind: "The artist is coming! The divinely favored, *der gottbegnadete* artist is coming!"

On the threshold of a shop that sold only Oriental wares—silks, vases, idols (who needed all that at the seaside?)—stood an ordinary untanned little man who followed with his dark eyes the promenaders as he waited in vain for a customer. Whom did he resemble? Yes, poor old Sarah's sick husband.

In the café where he presently joined our two farcical schemers, Martha was brought the wrong pastry and flew into a rage; for a long time she called to the overworked waiter, a mere boy, while the pastry (a splendid cream-oozing éclair) lay on its plate, lonely, despised, unwanted.

Less than a week had passed, and several times already that tender melancholy had come over Dreyer. True, he had experienced it before ("the melting heart of an egotist," Erica had once called it, adding: "You can hurt people or humiliate them, you are touched not by the blind man but by his dog"); but of late the melancholy had become less tender, or the tenderness more demanding. Perhaps it was the sun that had softened him up or maybe he was growing old, losing maybe something, and coming to resemble in some obscure way the pictureman whose services no one wanted and whose cry the children mocked.

When he went to bed that night he could not go to sleep —an unusual occurrence. On the previous day the sun, under the pretense of a caress, had so mutilated his back that he yearned for a spell of dull weather. They had been playing plop-catch, standing in the water up to their hips, Martha, Franz, two other young men, one of them a dancing instructor, the other a college student, the son of a Leipzig furrier. The dancing instructor had knocked Franz's blue glasses off with the ball, and the glasses had nearly drowned. Afterwards Franz and Martha had swum far out. He had stood and watched from the beach, cursing his lack of buoyancy. He borrowed a telescope from a kind ten-year-old stranger and for quite a while had kept an envious round eye on the two dark heads bobbing side by side in their blue safe round world. As soon as his back healed, he thought, he would start to take lessons in the hotel pool. Ouch, really burns! Impossible to find a painless position. Wooing sleep, he lay with closed eyes and saw the circular moat they had been digging to make their beach booth stand more cozily; he saw the tensed hairy leg of Franz digging nearby; then, the impossibly bright page of the verse anthology he had

[235]

tried to read as he lay in the sun. Oh, how it burns! Martha had promised it would get well tomorrow, definitely, would never hurt again. Yes, of course, the skin would grow stronger. Skin or no skin, I must win that bet tomorrow. Silly bet. Women can measure distances in centimeters, up skirts and down sleeves, but not leagues of water or miles of sand, or the upright glare of a door ajar. He turned over to the wall and in order to put himself asleep (not realizing how drowsy he was already despite the upright glare now between his shoulders) he began to repeat in his mind their sunset walk to Rockpoint. She liked bets and boats. She had maintained that a rowing-boat would make it faster there than a man on foot—even a man whose back burned in each of the four positions. He re-assumed the initial one, facing her door, and started to walk westward again but this time alone—she was in the other bedroom, and had not yet put out her light. If one walked westward with the slit of the sun in one's eyes along the bay after leaving the populated part of the beach, one found that the sandy strip between the heath on your left and the sea on your right gradually narrowed until your progress was stopped by an agony of jumbled rocks. I think I shall turn . . . good God. . . .

If instead of following the concave brink of the bay one takes a concentric path slightly inland as I am doing now, Rockpoint is reachable, I think, in twenty minutes or less, let us rearrange our left arm . . . how much more comfortable a limbless sleeper would be . . . and here is that path leading west from the poor back of the hotel. I traverse a hamlet and continue through a beech grove for a couple of kilometers. How quiet, how soft. . . . He stopped to rest on a bed in the grove but then gave a start and again saw the vertical line of burning pain.

He continued his wager walk. Oh, he must hurry. Or was

his pedometer slow? Or was that aspirin working at last? He emerged from the woods into heather, and presently the path, turning right, with a change of pillow, joined the coastline again at the spur called Rockpoint. Here one could stop and wait for the absurd little boat with Martha rowing like mad and enjoy the view. He enjoyed the view. He heard himself emitting a hippopotamian snore and regained consciousness. Rockpoint was a lonely little promontory, but she would come to one's bed if one won the bet. On one's right. . . . He rolled onto his right side and stopped hearing his heart. That's better. Aspirin comes from *sperare, speculum, spiegel*. Now he could see the sweep of the beach parallel to the trail one had followed, and followed, and followed. That shimmer over there, beyond a tiny rocky island, three kilometers east as the acrobat flies, was our stretch of the Gravitz beach with the sugar lumps of hotels. The little black boat with Martha in black evening dress, her eardrops blazing, had to skirt of course that little black island on the outside but otherwise geometrically speaking the seaway was shorter, the string of the bow, the sting of the bay, though even so, even a weary walker. . . .

When finally her husband's snore found a permanent rhythm, Martha got up, closed the door, and went back to her uncomfortable bed—it was much too soft and too far from the window which was open: beyond, there rose a steady soft incessant noise as if the black garden were a bath being run. Alas, it was not the sounding sea but the rain. Never mind, rain or no rain. Let him take an umbrella.

She put out the light, but it was no use trying to sleep. She stepped with Franz into the fatal bark, and he rowed her to the promontory. The process that had put her husband to sleep kept her awake. The rustle of the rain mingled with the buzz in her ears. Two hours passed—it was a much longer journey than anybody could have expected. She picked up her watch from the bed table and pondered its phosphorescent information. The sun was still in Siberia.

At half past seven Franz stirred. He had been told to get up at exactly half past seven. It was exactly half past seven. A baker in the encyclopedia who had poisoned an entire parish told the prison barber who was shaving his neck that never in his life had he slept so well. Franz had slept nine hours. His own contribution to the murder was up to now an accurate calculation of the distance to Rockpoint by land and by sea. The victim had to be there a few minutes before the boat arrived. He would be dead tired and grateful to be ferried back.

Franz opened his window, which faced south with no sea to view, but at least it revealed a small balcony one story lower on which on three consecutive afternoons at the siesta hour he had watched the spread-eagled barmaid sunning herself on a towel. The floor of the balcony was darkly damp. It might dry in time for her siesta if the sun came out before noon. "By this evening it will all be over," he reflected mechanically and was unable to imagine either that evening or the following day, as one is unable to imagine eternity.

Gritting his teeth he pulled on his clammy bathing trunks. The pockets of his robe were full of sand. He softly closed the door behind him and set out along the long white corridors. There was sand also in the toes of his canvas shoes, producing there a blunt blind sensation. His uncle and aunt were already sitting on their balcony having coffee. It was a sunless day, with a white sky, a gray sea, and a cheerless breeze. Aunt Martha poured Franz some coffee. She was also wearing her robe over a bathing suit. Green designs ran across the fluffy dark blue. She held back the broad sleeve with her free hand as she passed the cup to Franz.

Dreyer in blazer and flannel pants was reading the resort's guest list, occasionally pronouncing aloud a funny name. He had intended to wear a delicate pale-lemon Chinese tie that had cost fifty marks but Martha said it looked like rain and the tie would be ruined. So he had put on another, an old lavender one. In such trifles Martha usually was right. Dreyer drank two cups of coffee and enjoyed a roll with delicious transparent honey trickling over the edges. Martha drank three cups and did not eat anything. Franz had half a cup and ate nothing either. The wind swept across the balcony.

"Professor Klister of Swister," read Dreyer. "Sorry. Lister of Swistok."

"If you're finished, let's go," said Martha.

"Blavdak Vinomori," read Dreyer triumphantly.

"Let's go," said Martha, wrapping her robe around her and trying to keep her teeth from chattering. "Before it starts raining again."

"It's so early, my love," he drawled, casting a furtive glance at the plate of rolls. "Why does nobody at home ever give butter that curly shape?"

"Let's go," repeated Martha, rising. Franz got up also. Dreyer looked at his golden watch.

"I'll beat you anyway," he said gleefully. "You two go on ahead. I'll give you fifteen minutes. I could spare even more."

"Fine," said Martha.

"We'll see who wins," said Dreyer.

"We'll see," said Martha.

"Your oars or my calves," said Dreyer.

"Let me through, I can't get out," she exclaimed sharply, pushing with her knee and still fumbling at her robe.

Dreyer moved his chair, she passed.

"My back is much better," he said, "but Franz is seasick or something."

Franz, without looking at him, shook his head. With sunglasses over his usual spectacles and his bright red robe he looked like Blavdak Vinomori should look.

"Don't get drowned, Blavdak," said Dreyer and began his second roll.

The glass door closed. Chewing, and sucking his honey-smeared fingers, Dreyer considered with disapproval the big pale sea. A bit of beach was visible from the balcony, with its striped shelter boxes untidily scattered and slightly askew. He did not envy the hardy bathers. The spot where one rented boats was a little farther to the west, near the pier, and could not be seen from the balcony. An old man dressed like an opera captain let them. How chilly, soggy, and uninteresting everything was without the sun. Never mind. It would be a brisk bracing walk. As in the old days, the very old days, Martha had agreed to play with him a little and had not refused at the last minute because of the bad weather as he had secretly feared.

He looked again at his watch. Yesterday and the day before his office had called precisely at this time. Today, more than likely, Sarah would telephone again. He would call her back later. It was not worth waiting.

He wiped his lips firmly, brushed the crumbs off his lap, and went to the bathroom. That cold shower had been agony but now he felt fine. He paused before the mirror and ran his little silver brush right and left over his English mustache. His German nose was peeling. Not very attractive. A knock at the door.

The office had managed to catch him. Dreyer, beating his pocket, hurried to the telephone. The talk was brief. He wavered—should he take an umbrella—decided he would not and went out by the back entrance.

The two young fellows whom they had met yesterday were sitting sideways on a bench playing chess. Both held their legs crossed. White had his hand ensconced between the knee of the left leg and the calf of the other leg and dangled his right foot slightly. Black's arms were folded on his breast. Their gaze left the board as they greeted Dreyer. He stopped for a moment and gaily warned White that Black's knight was planning to attack White's king and queen with a forked check. Martha, who loved bets but thought them undignified, had asked him not to tell anybody about their little rendezvous at Rockpoint, so he said nothing about it and went on his way. "Old idiot," muttered Black, whose position was desperate.

Dreyer followed a boulevard of sorts, then a path, then walked through the hamlet where he observed that the bus to Swistok was leaving the post office and looked at his watch. It would catch the express to Berlin. As he turned right to rejoin the coastline, he glimpsed the sea and saw the speck of a boat in the blurry distance. He thought he distinguished two bright bathrobes but was not sure, and, quickening his step almost to a trot, entered the beechwood.

Franz rowed in silence, now grimly lowering his face, then in a sweep of despair turning it skyward. Martha sat at the helm. Before renting the boat, she had gone in the water for a minute, thinking it would warm her up. That had been a mistake. The sun that had made a half-promise had not kept it. The cold wet suit now stuck to her chest, hips, and sides. She was too excited and happy to pay much attention to such trifles. A delightfully compliant mist veiled the receding beach. The boat started to round the little rocky island where seagulls were the only witnesses. The oarlocks creaked ponderously.

"You don't want to ask anything, you remember everything, darling?"

Leaning forward on the back stroke, Franz nodded. And again stared at the empty sky as he pushed the resilient water.

". . . when I say, only when I say—remember?"

Another grim nod.

"Let us go over it quickly—all right? You remain in the bow—"

The oarlocks creaked, an inquisitive gull circled over them, a wave lifted the boat to inspect it. Franz bowed in answer. He tried not to look at his insane aunt but whether he stared at the damp bottom of the boat along which lay a second pair of oars or followed the happy seagull with his eyes, he nevertheless perceived Martha with his entire being and saw, even without looking, her rubber cap, her broad-jawed dreadful face, her shaven shins, her heavy coronation robes. And he knew exactly how it would all be, how Martha would cry out the password, how both rowers would stand up to change places . . . the boat would rock . . . not easy to get past each other . . . careful . . . one more step . . . nearer . . . now!

". . . remember—just one big push, with your whole body," said Martha, and he slowly bent forward again.

"You must send him flying out, toppling in, face forward, and then you row like hell."

Now a chill breeze was penetrating her body with dampness and yet the elation persisted. She gazed intently at the in-curved shore, at its fringe of forest, at the mauve stretch of heather, searching for the place, near a pointed rock, where they were to land. She saw it. She pulled taut the left rope of the rudder.

Franz, as he swung backwards with a soundless moan, heard Martha laugh hoarsely, cough, clear her throat, cough, and laugh again. A sizable wave took possession of the boat. He stopped rowing for a moment. The sweat trickled down his temples in spite of the cold. Martha rose and fell with the wave's motion, shivering, aged beyond belief, her gray face shining like rubber.

She was watching a tiny dark figure that had suddenly appeared on the deserted strip of jutting land.

"Quicker," she said, trembling and plucking at the icy-cold clinging bathing suit as if it were a sheet, and she dying. "Oh, please! He's waiting."

Franz laid down the oars, slowly took off both pairs of glasses, slowly wiped the lenses of both on the flap of his robe.

"I told you to hurry!" she shouted. "You don't need those silly sunglasses. Franz, do you hear?"

He put the sunglasses into the pocket of his robe. He raised the other pair skyward. He looked through the lenses at the clouds; then he slowly put them on and took up the oars again.

The dark little figure became more distinct and acquired a face like a grain of maize. Martha was moving her torso back and forth, perhaps repeating Franz's movements, perhaps trying to speed up the boat.

Now the blue jacket and gray pants were distinguishable. He stood with his feet planted apart and his arms akimbo.

"This is the critical moment," said Martha, already speaking in a whisper. "He will never get into a boat if he does not now. Try to look more cheerful."

She was twisting the end of the rudder ropes in her hands. The shore was drawing near.

Dreyer stood looking at them and smiling. In his palm he held a flat gold watch. He had arrived eight minutes ahead of them, eight whole minutes. The boat was called "Lindy." Cute.

"Welcome," he said, putting the watch back in his pocket.

"You must have run all the way," said Martha, breathing heavily and glancing around.

"Nothing of the sort. Took it easy. Even stopped to rest along the way."

She continued her survey. Sand, rocks, and further on, heathery slopes and woods. Not a soul, not a dog ever came here.

"Get into the boat," she said.

Lapping little waves jolted the boat ever so slightly. Franz was listlessly fussing with the second pair of oars.

Dreyer said: "Oh, I'll return the same way. It's wonderful in the woods. I made friends with a squirrel. We'll meet at the Siren Café."

"Get in," she repeated sharply. "You can row a little. You're getting fat. Look how tired Franz is. I can't row alone."

"Really, my love, I don't feel like it at all. I hate rowing, and my back smarts again."

"All right," she said, "it was part of the bet and if you don't get in at once, I'm not playing, the bet is cancelled."

Martha was slapping her palm with the rudder rope. He rolled up his eyes, sighed and, trying not to wet his feet, started awkwardly, cautiously, to get into the boat. "Illogical and unfair," he said, and fell down heavily in the middle seat.

The second pair of oars were in the locks. Dreyer took off his blazer. The boat moved off.

A sense of blissful peace now descended on Martha. The plan had worked, the dream had come true. A deserted beach, a deserted sea, and fog. Just to be safe they should go out some distance north of the shore. An odd, cool, not unpleasant emptiness was in her chest and head as if the breeze had blown right through her, cleaning her inwardly, removing all the trash. And through that cool vibration she heard his carefree voice.

"You keep getting tangled up in my oars, Franz—that's no way to row. You have never rowed in your life, I suspect. Of course, I can understand that your thoughts are far away. . . . There again. You must pay a little more attention to what I'm trying to do. Together, together! She hasn't forgotten you. I hope you left her your address. One, two. I'm positive there'll be a letter for you today saying she's with child. Rhythm! Rhythm!"

Franz watched his firm stout neck, the yellow strands of hair thinning on pink suede, the white shirt now growing taut on his back, then ballooning. But he saw it all as if through a dream.

"Ah, children, it was glorious in the woods," the voice was saying. "The beeches, the gloom, the bindweed. Keep in rhythm!"

Martha, through half-closed eyes, was looking with interest at this face which she was seeing for the last time. Beside her lay his blazer; it contained the golden timepiece, the silver mustache brush, and a plump wallet. She was glad these things would not be lost. A little bonus. Somehow, she did not realize at that moment that the jacket with its contents would have to be thrown in the water too. This rather complicated question arose only later when the main matter had already been settled. Now her thoughts were circling slowly, almost languidly. The anticipation of hard-won happiness was ravishing.

"I must admit I was wrong in thinking this would irritate my back. You promised, darling, it would be all right today, and sure enough it's much better. Remember, I've won the bet. And I can row a hundred times better than that rascal behind me. My shirt keeps rubbing the itchy spots, and that feels good. I think I shall take off my tie."

They were now sufficiently far from the shore. It was drizzling. A number of white spectators had found their seats on their black island. The tie joined the blazer. The wavelets broke and foamed around the boat.

"Actually, it's my last day," said Dreyer, energetically rowing.

That tragic pronouncement left Franz unmoved; there was already nothing in the world that could shock him. Martha, however, gave her husband a curious glance. Premonitions, eh?

"I have to leave for the city early tomorrow," he explained. "I just had a call."

The rain was growing stronger. Martha glanced around, then looked at Franz. They could begin.

"Listen, Kurt," she said quietly, "I feel like rowing a bit. You take Franz's place, and Franz will steer."

"No, wait, my love," said Dreyer, trying to do as Franz was doing—to flatten his oars over the water, swallow-like on the backstroke. "I'm just getting warmed up. Franz and I have got our rhythm synchronized. His form is improving. Sorry, my love—I think I splashed you."

"I'm cold," said Martha. "Please get up and let me row."

"Five more minutes," said Dreyer, trying again to feather his oars, and again failing.

Martha shrugged. The sensation of power was ecstatic; she was willing to prolong that sensation.

"Eight more strokes," she said with a smile. "The years of our marriage. I'll count."

"Come on, don't spoil it. We'll let you row soon. After all, I'm leaving tomorrow."

He felt hurt that she was not interested to know why he had to go. She must think it was just a routine trip, some ordinary office business.

"An amusing surprise," he said casually.

She was moving her lips with singular concentration.

"Tomorrow," he said, "I'm making a hundred thousand dollars at one stroke."

Martha, who had got to the end of her count, raised her head.

"I'm selling an extraordinary patent. That's the kind of business we are doing."

Franz suddenly laid down his oars and began wiping his glasses. For some reason he thought Dreyer was talking to him and as he wiped the sweat and the rain away, he nodded and cleared his throat. Actually he had reached a stage at which human speech, unless representing a command, was meaningless.

"You didn't think I was so smart, eh?" said Dreyer, who had also stopped rowing. "At one stroke—just think!"

"I suppose this is one of your jokes," she said, frowning.

"Word of honor," he said plaintively. "I'm the sole owner of a miraculous invention, and I'm going to sell it to Mr. Ritter, whom you know."

"What is it—some kind of trouser press?"

He shook his head.

"Something to do with sports, with tennis?"

"It's a big glorious secret," he said, "and you're a goose not to believe me."

She turned away, biting her chapped underlip, and stared for a long time at the inky horizon, where a gray fringe of rain hung against a narrow light-colored band of sky.

"You're sure it's a hundred thousand dollars? Is that definite?"

It was not, but he nodded, and pulled at the oars, hearing that the rower behind him had resumed his work.

"Can't you tell me a little more?" she asked, still looking away. "You're sure it won't drag on? You'll have that money in a few days?"

"Why yes, I hope so. And I'll come back here and we'll go rowing again. And Franz will teach me to swim."

"It can't be; you're deceiving me," she cried.

Dreyer started to laugh, not understanding why she chose not to believe him.

"I shall return with a great bag of gold," he said. "Like a medieval merchant back from Bagdad on a donkey. Oh, I'm pretty certain I'll clinch that deal tomorrow."

The rain would stop one moment and the next start pouring again, as if practicing. Dreyer, noticing how far out they had gone, began turning the boat with his right oar; Franz mechanically backed water with his left. Martha sat lost in thought, now consulting the filling of a back tooth with her tongue, now running it over her lips. Presently Dreyer offered to let her row. She gave a silent shake of her head.

The rain now came down in earnest, and Dreyer felt its soothing coolness through the raw silk of his shirt. He tingled with vigor, this was great fun, with every stroke he rowed better. The shore appeared through the mist; one could make out the flags and the striped shelters; the long pier was beginning slowly and carefully to take aim at the moving target of their boat.

"So you'll be back Saturday, not later than Saturday?" asked Martha.

Franz could see, through Dreyer's soaked shirt, flesh-colored patches which showed now here, now there, a geography of hideous pink, depending on which country adhered to the skin in the process of rowing.

"Saturday or Sunday," Dreyer said zestfully and, as the surf adopted him, caught a crab.

The rain lashed down. Martha's robe enveloped her in heavy humidity that made her ribs ache. What could she care about neuralgia, bronchitis, irregular heart beat? She was entirely immersed in the question—was she doing the right thing or not. Yes, she was. Yes, the sun would again shine. They would go boating again, now that he had discovered this new sport. Every now and then she would glance past her husband at Franz. He must be perplexed and disappointed, poor pet. He is tired. His poor mouth is open. My baby! Never mind, we'll soon be back, and you'll rest, and I'll bring you some brandy, and we'll lock the door.

"Lindy" was returned intact. Bending their heads under the fierce downpour, our three holidayers walked across soggy dark sand and then up slippery steps to the desolate promenade. When they finally reached their apartment, Martha was unpleasantly surprised to find her door open. The two maids she disliked most, one a thief, the other a slut, were busy, too busy, making her room, which she had told them to do always *punkt* at ten, and now it was almost noon. But a strange apathy weighed upon her. She said nothing, and went to wait in Dreyer's bedroom. There she pulled off her heavy robe and sank into an armchair, feeling too tired to peel off her bathing suit and get a towel from the bathroom. Anyway, her husband was in the bathroom; she saw him through the open door. Naked, full of ruddy life, various parts of his anatomy leaping, he was giving himself a robust rub-down, and helling every time he touched his red-blotched shoulders. One of the girls knocked to say Madam's room was ready, and Martha had to make a great effort in order to undertake the long journey into the next room.

She washed and dressed—with infinite intervals of languor. A turtleneck thick red sweater which Franz had lent her on the esplanade the night before—or was it two nights? —looked a little too masculine but it was the warmest thing she could find. However, it hardly muffled the fits of shivering that kept tormenting her body, while her mind was enjoying such peace, such euphoria. Of course, she had done the right thing. Moreover, the dress rehearsal had gone perfectly. Everything was under control.

"Everything is under control," said Dreyer through the door. "I hope you are as hungry as I am. We'll have lunch in the grill in ten minutes. I'll be waiting for you in the reading room."

All she could envisage was a cup of black coffee, and a little brandy. When her husband had gone, she stepped across the corridor and knocked at Franz's door. It was unlocked, the room was empty. His robe sprawled on the floor, and there were other untidy details, but she did not have the strength to do anything about it. She found him in a corner of the lounge. The barmaid, a skinny artificial blonde, was bothering him with vulgar small talk.

Meanwhile the rain did not cease. The needle that marked on a roll the violet graph of atmospheric pressure acquired a sacred significance. People on the promenade approached it as they would a crystal ball. Its competitor in the gallery, a conservative barometer, also refused to be propitiated either by prayer or knuckleknock. Someone had forgotten a little red pail on the beach and it was already filled to the brim with rain water. The photographers moped; the restaurateurs rejoiced. One could find all the same faces now in one café, now in another. Toward evening the rain thinned, and then stopped. Dreyer held his breath as he made carom shots. The word spread that the needle had risen one millimeter. "Fine weather tomorrow," said a prophet, expressively striking his palm with his fist. Red at night, sailor's delight. Despite the cool air, many dined on public verandas. The evening mail arrived: a major event. On the promenade the after-dinner shuffling of many feet began under the lights, bemisted by the damp. There was dancing at the *kursaal*.

In the afternoon, she had lain down under a quilt and two blankets; but the chill endured. For supper she could eat only a pickle and a couple of pale cooked cherries. Now, in the Tanz Salon, she felt a stranger to the icy noise around. The black petals of her vaporous dress did not seem right, as if they would come apart at any moment. The tight touch of silk on her calves and the strip of garter along her bare thigh were infernal contacts. A colored snowstorm of confetti left its flakes sticking to her bare back, and at the same time, limbs and spine did not belong to her. A pain, of another musical tone than intercostal neuralgia or that strange ache which a great cardiologist had told her came from a "shadow behind the heart," entered into excruciating concords with the orchestra. The dance rhythm did not lull or delight her as it usually did, but, instead, traced an angular line, the graph of her fever, along the surface of her skin. With every movement of her head, a compact pain rolled like a bowling ball from temple to temple. At one of the best tables around the hall, she had for a right-hand neighbor the dance instructor, a famous young man who flitted all summer from resort to resort like a velvet butterfly; on her left was Schwarz, the dark-eyed student, son of a Leipzig millionaire. The slipper under the table had apparently been kicked off by her. She heard Martha Dreyer ask questions, supply answers, comment on the horror of the thundering hall. The fizzy little stars of champagne pricked an unfamiliar tongue, without warming her blood or quenching her thirst. With an invisible hand she took Martha by the left wrist and felt her pulse. It was not there, however, but somewhere behind her ear or in the neck, or in the grinning instruments of the band, or in Franz and Dreyer, sitting opposite her. All around, growing from the hands of the dancers, glossy blue, red, green balloons bobbed on long strings and each contained the entire ballroom, and the chandeliers, and the tables, and herself. The tight embrace of the foxtrot engendered no heat in her body. She noticed that Martha was dancing also, holding high a green world. Her partner in full erection against her leg was declaring his love in panting sentences from some lewd book. Again the stars of champagne crept upwards, and the balloons resumed their bobbing, and again most of Martha's leg was in Weiss's crotch, and he moaned as his cheek touched hers, and his fingers explored her naked back.

She was sitting again at the table. Red, blue, green spots were swimming in Franz's glasses. Dreyer was guffawing vulgarly slapping the table with his palm and leaning back. She extended her foot beneath the table and pressed. Franz gave a start, stood up, and bowed. She placed her hand on his dear bony shoulder. How happy they had been in the rhythm of that earlier novel in those first chapters, under the picture of the dancing slave girl between the whirling dervishes. For one delicious moment the music pierced her private fog, reached her, enveloped her. Everything was fine again, for this was he, Franz, his shy hands, his breath, the soft fuzz on the back of his neck, under her fingernails, and those precious, adorable motions that *she* had taught him.

"Closer, closer," she murmured. "Make me feel warm."

"I'm tired," he murmured back. "I'm tired to death. Please don't do what you are doing, please."

The music reared its trumpets and then collapsed. Franz followed her back to the table. People around her were clapping. The dancing instructor slipped past her with a bright-yellow girl. Walnut-brown Mr. Vinomori, the iris brimming meaningfully in the white of his eyes, was bowing to her, enticing. She saw Martha Dreyer nestle up to him and begin a tango.

Uncle and nephew remained sitting alone. Dreyer was beating time with his finger, watching the dancers, waiting for the recurrent return of his wife's green earrings, and, with a kind of awe, listening to the strong voice of a girl singer. Stocky and joyless, she bawled out, straining her throat and prancing in time to the music: "Montevideo, Montevideo is not the right place for *meinen Leo*." She was jostled by the dancers; endlessly she repeated the ear-splitting refrain; a fat man in tuxedo, her owner, hissed at her, telling her to choose some other song because nobody was enjoying it; Dreyer had heard this *Montevideo* both yesterday and the day before, and he was again filled with a bizarre melancholy, and felt embarrassed for the poor dumpy girl when her voice cracked on a note and she recovered the tune with a brave smile. Franz sat beside him, shoulder to shoulder, and seemed also to be watching the dancers. He was a little drunk and his muscles ached from that morning rowing. He felt like letting his forehead fall onto the table to remain thus forever, between a full ashtray and an empty bottle. A reptile, a supple dragon was tormenting him elaborately and hideously, turning him inside out—and there was no end to that torment. A human being, and after all he was a human being, was not supposed to go on enduring such oppression.

It was at that moment that Franz regained consciousness like an insufficiently drugged patient on the operating table. As he came to, he knew he was being cut open, and he would have howled horribly if he were not in an invented ballroom. He looked around, toying with the string of a balloon tied to a bottle. He saw, reflected in a rococo mirror, the meek back of Dreyer's head nodding in time to the music.

Franz looked away; his gaze became entangled amid the legs of the dancers and attached itself desperately to a gleaming blue dress. The foreign girl in the blue dress danced with a remarkably handsome man in an old-fashioned dinner jacket. Franz had long since noticed this couple; they had appeared to him in fleeting glimpses, like a recurrent dream image or a subtle leitmotiv—now at the beach, now in a café, now on the promenade. Sometimes the man carried a butterfly net. The girl had a delicately painted mouth and tender gray-blue eyes, and her fiancé or husband, slender, elegantly balding, contemptuous of everything on earth but her, was looking at her with pride; and Franz felt envious of that unusual pair, so envious that his oppression, one is sorry to say, grew even more bitter, and the music stopped. They walked past him. They were speaking loudly. They were speaking a totally incomprehensible language.

"Your aunt dances like a goddess," said the student, sitting down beside him.

"I'm very tired," remarked Franz irrelevantly. "I rowed a lot today. Rowing is a very healthy sport."

Meanwhile Dreyer was saying with an ingratiating wink: "Am I also permitted to invite you for a dance? If I promise not to tread on your feet?"

"Get me out of here," said Martha. "I'm not feeling well."

13

Barely awake and still blinking, his yellow pajamas unbuttoned on his pink stomach, Dreyer went out on the balcony. The wet foliage scintillated blindingly. The sea was milky-bluish, sparked with silver. On the adjacent balcony his wife's bathing suit was drying. He returned to his darkish bedroom, in a hurry to dress and leave for Berlin. At eight o'clock there was a bus that took forty minutes to reach Swistok and its railway; a taxi would bring him there in less than half an hour to catch an earlier train. He tried not to sing under the shower so as not to disturb neighbors. He had an enjoyable shave on the balcony in front of an absolutely stable and unbreakable new type of mirror screwed onto the balustrade. Diving back into the penumbra, he briskly dressed.

Very softly he opened the door into the adjacent bedroom. From the bed came Martha's rapid voice: "We're going to a tombola in a gondola. Please hurry."

She often talked in her sleep babbling about Franz, Frieda, Oriental gymnastics.

As he slapped his sides to check if he had distributed

everything among the proper pockets, Dreyer laughed and said: "Good-by, my love. I'm leaving for the city."

She muttered something in a waking voice, then said distinctly: "Give me some water."

"I'm in a hurry," he said. "You get it yourself. Okay? Time for you to go swimming with Franz. Heavenly morning."

He bent over the dark bed, kissed her hair and walked through his own bedroom into the long corridor leading to the lift.

He had his coffee on the Kurhaus terrace. He had two rolls with butter and honey. He consulted his watch and ate a third. On the beach one could see the bright robes of early swimmers and the sea was growing more and more luminous. He lit a cigarette and popped into the taxi that the concierge had called.

The sea was left behind. By that time a few more bathers were dotting the flashing green-blue. From every balcony came the delicate tinkle of breakfast. Automatically tucking a hateful ball under his arm, Franz marched down the corridor and knocked at Martha's door. Silence. The door was locked. He knocked at Dreyer's door, entered and found his uncle's room in disorder. He concluded, correctly, that Dreyer had already left for Berlin. A terrible day was in store. The door into Martha's room was ajar. It was dark there. Let her sleep. This was good. He started to tiptoe away but from the darkness came Martha's voice: "Why don't you give me that water?" she said with listless insistence.

Franz located a decanter and a glass and moved toward the bed. Martha slowly raised herself, freed a bare arm, and drank avidly. He put the decanter back on the dresser and was about to resume his stealthy retreat.

"Franz, come here," she called in that same toneless voice.

He sat down on the edge of her bed, grimly expecting she would command him to fulfill a duty that he had managed to evade since they came here.

"I think I am very ill," she said pensively, not raising her head from the pillow.

"Let me ring for your coffee," said Franz. "It's sunny today and here it's so dark."

She began to speak again. "He's used up all the aspirin. Go to the pharmacy and get me some. And tell them to take that oar away—it keeps hurting me."

"Oar? That's your hot-water bottle. What's the matter with you?"

"Please, Franz. I can't speak. And I'm cold. I need lots of blankets."

He brought one from Dreyer's room, and clumsily, carelessly, fuming at a woman's whim, covered her with it.

"I don't know where the pharmacy is," he said.

Martha asked: "You brought it? What have you brought?"

He shrugged and went out.

He found the pharmacy without difficulty. Besides the aspirin tablets he bought a tube of shaving cream and a postcard with a view of the bay. The package had safely arrived but Emmy wondered in her last letter if he was quite right in the head and he thought he'd send her a few words of protest and reassurance. As he walked back to the hotel along the sunny promenade, he stopped to look down at the beach. He had separated the aspirin container from the shaving cream which he now put into his pocket. A sudden breeze took possession of the paper baglet which had contained both. At that moment the puzzling foreign couple overtook him. They were both in beach robes and walked rapidly, rapidly conversing in their mysterious tongue. He thought that they glanced at him and fell silent for an instant. After passing him they began talking again; he had the impression they were discussing him, and even pronouncing his name. It embarrassed, it incensed him, that this damned happy foreigner hastening to the beach with his tanned, pale-haired, lovely companion, knew absolutely everything about his predicament and perhaps pitied, not without some derision, an honest young man who had been seduced and appropriated by an older woman who, despite her fine dresses and face lotions, resembled a large white toad. And generally speaking, tourists at these swanky resorts are always inquisitive, mocking, cruel people. He felt the shame of his hairy nudity barely concealed by the charlatan robe. He cursed the breeze and the sea and, clutching the container with the tablets, entered the lobby of his hotel. The flimsy paper he had lost fluttered along the promenade, settled, fluttered again, and slithered past the happy couple; then it was wafted toward a bench in an embrasure of the balustrade, where an old man sitting in the sun meditatively pierced it with the point of his cane. What happened to it next is not known. Those hurrying to the beach did not follow its fate. Wooden steps led down to the sand. One was anxious to reach the sea's slow shining folds. The white sand sung underfoot. Among a hundred similarly striped shelters it was easy to recognize one's own—and not only by the number it bore: those rentable objects grow accustomed to their chance owner remarkably fast, becoming part of his life simply and trustfully. Three or four shelters away was the Dreyers' niche; now it stood empty—neither Dreyer, nor his wife, nor his nephew was there. A huge rampart of sand surrounded it. A little boy in red trunks was climbing all over that rampart, and the sand trickled down, sparkling, and presently a whole chunk of it crumbled. Mrs. Dreyer would not have liked to see strange children ruining her fortress. Within its confines and around them the impatient elements had already had time to scramble the prints of bare feet. None could distinguish now Dreyer's robust imprint from Franz's narrow sole. A while later Schwarz and Weiss came over, saw with surprise that nobody was there yet. "Fascinating, adorable woman," one of them said, and the other looked across the beach at the promenade, at the hotels beyond it, and replied: "Oh, I'm sure they'll be down in a few minutes. Let's go for a swim and come back later." The shelter and its moat remained deserted. The little boy had run back to his sister who had brought a blue pailful of toy water and after magic manipulations and pattings was carefully shaking out of the pail an impeccably formed cone of chocolate sand. A white butterfly went by, battling the breeze. Flags flapped. The photographer's shout approached. Bathers entering the shallow water moved their legs like skiers without their poles.

And in the meantime a cluster of these seaside images—gleams on the green folding wave—were travelling south at fifty miles an hour comfortably collected in Dreyer's mind, and the further he travelled from the sea in the Berlin express, the more insistently they demanded attention. The foretaste of the affairs awaiting him in the city grew a little insipid at the thought that at the very moment he was being transformed again into a businessman with a businessman's schemes and fancies, and that there, by the sea, on the white sand of true reality, he was leaving freedom behind. And the closer he came to the metropolis, the more attractive seemed to him that shimmering *plage* that one could see like a mirage from Rockpoint.

At home, the gardener informed him of Tom's death: the dog, he thought, had been hit by a truck, it was found unconscious and had died, he said, in his arms. Dreyer gave him fifty marks for his sympathy, reflecting sadly that no-body besides that rather coarse old soldier had really loved the poor beast. At the office he learned that Mr. Ritter would meet him not in the lobby of the Adlerhof but at the bar of the Royal. Before going there, he rang up Isolda at her mother's at Spandau and pleaded abjectly for a brief date later in the evening, but Isolda said she was busy, and sug-gested he call her again tomorrow or the day after tomorrow and take her to the premiere of the film, *King, Queen, Knave,* and then one would see.

His American guest, a pleasant, cultured person with steel-gray hair and a triple chin, asked about Martha, whom he had met a couple of years before, and Dreyer was disap-pointed to discover that all the English learned since the day of that pleasant party was not sufficient to cope with the nasal pronunciation of Mr. Ritter—whereupon the latter courteously switched to an old-fashioned brand of German. Another disappointment awaited Dreyer at the "laboratory." Instead of the three automannequins promised him, only two were available for the show—the initial elderly gentle-man, wearing a replica of Dreyer's blue blazer, and a stiff-looking, bronze-wigged lady in a green dress with high cheekbones and a masculine chin.

"You might have thrown in a little more bosom," observed Dreyer reproachfully.

"Scandinavian type," said the Inventor.

"Scandinavian type," said Dreyer. "Female impersonator, rather."

"An amalgam, if you like. We ran into some trouble, a rib failed to function properly. After all, I need more time than God did, Mr. Director. But I'm sure you'll love the way her hips work."

"Another thing," said Dreyer. "I don't much care for the

old chap's necktie. You must have got it in Croatia or Liechtenstein. Anyway it is not one of those my store provided. In fact, I remember the one he had on last time; it was a beautiful light blue like yours."

Moritz and Max tittered.

"I confess," said the Inventor calmly, "to have borrowed it for this important occasion." He started to worry the front stud of the tall collar under his rustling beard, but before it could spring, Dreyer had already swished off his own pearl-gray tie and remained with an open shirt collar for the rest of his known existence.

Mr. Ritter was dozing in an armchair in the "theater." Dreyer coughed loudly. His guest woke up rubbing his eyes like a child. The show started.

Gyrating her angular hips, the woman passed across the stage more like a streetwalker than a sleepwalker. She was followed by the drunken viveur. Presently she jerked by again in a mink coat, reeled, recovered, completed her agonizing stretch, and the sound of a massive thud came from the wings. Her would-be client did not appear. There was a long pause.

"That meal you bought me was certainly something," said Mr. Ritter. "I'll have my revanche when madame and you visit me in Miami next spring. I have a Spanish chef who worked for years in a French restaurant in London so you do really get quite a cosmopolitan menu."

This time the woman drifted past on slow roller skates, in a black evening dress, her legs rigid, her profile like that of a skull, her décolleté revealing a tricot smudged by the hasty hands of her maker. His two accomplices failed to catch her behind the scenes where her brief career ended in an ominous clatter. There was another pause. Dreyer wondered what aberration of the mind had ever made him accept, let alone admire, those tipsy dummies. He hoped the end of the show had come but Mr. Ritter and he had not yet seen the best number.

White-gloved, in evening dress, one hand raised to his top hat, the old chap entered, looking refreshed and gay. He stopped in front of the spectators and started to remove his hat in a complicated, much too complicated, salute. Something crunched.

"*Halt*," howled the Inventor with great presence of mind and darted toward the mechanical maniac. "Too late!" The hat was doffed with a flourish but the arm came off too.

A photographer's black curtain was mercifully drawn.

"*How have you liked?*" asked Dreyer in English.

"Fascinating," said Mr. Ritter and started to leave. "You'll hear from me in a couple of days. I have to decide, you see, which of two projects to finance.

"Is the other similar?"

"Oh, no. Oh, goodness, no. The other has to do with running water in luxury hotels. Water made to produce recognizable tunes. The music of water in a literal sense. An orchestra of faucets. Wash your hands in a barcarolla, bathe in *Lohengrin*, rinse your silver in Debussy."

"Or drown in a Bach," punned Dreyer.

He spent the rest of the evening at home, trying to read an English play called *Candida*, and every now and then lapsing into lazy thought. The automannequins had given all they could give. Alas, they had been pushed too far. Bluebeard had squandered his hypnotic force, and now they had lost all significance, all life and charm. He was grateful to them, in a vague sort of way, for the magical task they had performed, the excitement, the expectations. But they only disgusted him now.

He worked through another scene, dutifully leafing

through his dictionary at every stumble. He would ring up Isolda tomorrow. He would hire a pretty English girl to teach him the language of Shaw and Galsworthy. He would simply resell the invention to Bluebeard. Ah, brilliant idea! For a token sum of ten dollars.

How quiet the house was. No Tom, no Martha. She was not a good loser, poor girl. All at once he understood what subtle extra was added to the lifeless silence: all the clocks had stopped in the house.

A little after eleven he rose from his comfortable seat and was about to go up to the bedroom when the telephone placed a cold hand on his shoulder.

He was now speeding in a hired limousine driven by a broad-shouldered chauffeur through an infinite nocturnal expanse of woods and field, and northern towns, their names garbled by the impatient darkness—Nauesack, Wusterbeck, Pritzburg, Nebukow. Their weak lights fumbled at him in passing, the car shook and swayed, he had been promised they would make it in five hours, but they did not, and a gray morning was already abustle with bicycles weaving among crawling trucks when he reached Swistok, from which it was twenty miles to Gravitz.

The desk clerk, a dark-haired young man with hollow cheeks and big glasses, informed him that one of their guests happened to be Professor Lister of international fame; he had visited Madame last night, and was with her now.

As Dreyer strode toward his apartment, the doctor, a tall bald old man in a monastic-looking dressing gown with a brown satchel under his arm, came out of Martha's room. "It is unheard-of," he growled at Dreyer without bothering to shake hands with him. "A woman has pneumonia with a temperature of 106 and nobody bothers. Her husband leaves her in that state and goes for a trip. Her nephew is a nincompoop. If a maid had not alerted me last night you would be still carousing in Berlin."

"So the situation is serious," said Dreyer.

"Serious? The respiratory count is fifty. The heart behaves fantastically. It is not a normal organ for a woman of twenty-nine."

"Thirty-four," said Dreyer. "There is a mistake in her passport."

"Or thirty-four. Anyway, she should be transported at once to the Swistok clinic where I can have her treated adequately."

"Yes, at once," said Dreyer.

The old man nodded crossly and swept away. One of the maids Martha disliked, the one who had stolen at least three handkerchiefs in as many days, was now dressed as a nurse (she had worked in winter at the clinic).

Plain brown or the heather tweed? Franz on the terrace of a café was in the middle of a nervous yawn when the doctor billowed past, heading for a quick swim before going to Swistok. Plain brown. Gruff Lister could not help being touched by the young fellow's dejection and shouted to him from the promenade: "Your uncle is here."

Franz went up to Dreyer's room and stood listening to the moaning and muttering in the adjacent room. Would fate allow her to divulge their secrets? He knocked very lightly on the door. Dreyer came out of the sickroom, and he likewise was touched by Franz's distraught appearance. Presently from the balcony they saw the ambulance enter the drive.

Over the waves, small angular waves, that rose and fell in time to her breathing, Martha floated in a white boat, and at the oars sat Dreyer and Franz. Franz smiled at her over Dreyer's bent head, and she saw her gay parasol reflected in

the happy gleam of his glasses. Franz was wearing one of the
long nightshirts that had belonged to his father, and continued to smile at her expectantly as the boat dipped and
creaked as if on springs. And Martha said: "It's time. We can
begin." Dreyer stood up, Franz stood up also, and both
reeled, laughing heartily, locked in an involuntary embrace.
Franz's long shirt rippled in the wind, and now he was
standing alone, still laughing and swaying, and out of the
water a hand protruded. "Take the oar, hit him," cried
Martha, choking with laughter. Franz, standing firmly on
the blue glass of the water, raised the oar, and the hand
disappeared. They were now alone in the boat, which was
no longer a boat but a café with one large marble table, and
Franz was sitting opposite her, and his odd attire had ceased
to matter. They were drinking beer (how thirsty she was).
Franz shared her unsteady glass while Dreyer kept slapping
the table with his wallet to summon the waiter. "Now," she
said, and Franz said something in Dreyer's ear, and Dreyer got
up, laughing, and they both went away. While Martha waited
her chair rose and fell, it was a floating café. Franz came back
alone carrying her late husband's blue jacket over his arm;
he nodded to her significantly and tossed it on the empty
chair. Martha wanted to kiss Franz but the table separated
them and the marble edge bit into her chest. Coffee was
brought—three pots, three cups—and it took her some time
to realize there was one portion too many. The coffee was
too hot, so she decided that since a drizzle had set in, it was
best to wait for the rain to dilute the coffee, but the rain
was hot too and Franz kept urging her to go home, pointing at
their villa across the road. "Let's begin," she said. All three
got up, and Dreyer, pale and sweaty, started to pull on his
blue jacket. That perturbed her. It was dishonest, it was
illegal. She gestured in mute indignation. Franz understood

and, talking to him firmly, began leading away Dreyer, who staggered as he fumbled for the armhole of his blazer. Franz returned alone but no sooner had he sat down than Dreyer appeared from another direction, furtively making his way back, and his face was now utterly ghastly and inadmissible. With a sidelong glance at her he shook his head and seated himself without a word at the oars of the bed. Martha was overcome by such impatience that as soon as the bed began to move she screamed. The new boat rode through long corridors. She wanted to stand up but an oar blocked her way. Franz rowed steadily. Something kept telling her that not all had been properly done. She remembered—the jacket! The blue jacket lay at the bottom of the boat, its arms looked empty but the back was not flat enough, in fact it bulged, it humped suspiciously, and now the two sleeves were swelling. She saw the thing trying to rise on all fours, and grabbed it, and Franz and she swung it back and forth and hurled it out of the boat. But it would not sink. It slithered from wave to wave as if alive. She nudged it with an oar; it clutched at the oar, trying to clamber aboard. Franz reminded her that it still contained the watch, and the coat, now a blue mackintosh because of the water, slowly sank, limply moving its exhausted sleeves. They watched it disappear. Now the job was done, and an enormous, turbulent joy engulfed her. Now it was easy to breathe, that drink they had given her was a wonderful poison, Benedictine and bile, and her husband was already dressed, saying: "Hurry up, I'm taking you to a ball," but Franz had mislaid her jewels.

Before leaving with her for the hospital, Dreyer told Franz to hold the fort, they would be back in a few days. There was probably not much difference basically between Martha's delirium and her wretched lover's state of mind. Once, on the eve of a school examination, when he desperately needed a passing mark in order not to repeat a whole class year, a clever sly boy said to him there was a trick that always worked if you knew how to apply it. With the utmost clarity, with all the forces of your mind bunched up in an iron fist, you had to visualize not what you wanted, not the passing mark, not her death, not freedom, but the other possibility, failure, the absence of your name from the list of those who had passed, and a healthy, ravenous, implacable Martha returning to her merry seaside inferno to make him carry out the scheme they had postponed. But according to the boy's advice, that did not suffice: the really hard part of the trick was ignoring success utterly and naturally as if the very thought of it did not exist in one's mind. Franz could not recall if he had achieved that feat in the case of the examination (which eventually he did pass) but he knew that he was incapable of managing it now. No matter how distinctly he imagined the three of them sitting again on the terrace of the Marmora tavern, and renewing the wager, and again getting Dreyer into the boat, he would notice out of the corner of his eye that the boat had floated away without them and that Dreyer was telephoning from the hospital to say she was dead.

Going to the other extreme, he allowed himself the dangerous luxury of imagining the freedom, the ecstasy of freedom awaiting him. Then, after that awful volupty of thought, he tried other ways of tricking fate. He counted the boats for hire and added their sum to that of the number of people in the open-air café on the beach, telling himself that odd would mean death. The number was odd but now he wondered if somebody had not left or come while he counted.

The day before he had resolved to take advantage of solitude and make a purchase that Dreyer might have ridiculed